BILLIARDS AT THE H

DUŠAN ŠAROTAR

Billiards at the Hotel Dobray

Translated from the Slovene by
Rawley Grau

First published in 2019 by **Istros Books**
(in collaboration with Beletrina Academic Press)
London, United Kingdom
www.istrosbooks.com

Originally published in Slovene as *Biljard v Dobrayu* by Beletrina Academic Press, 2007

Translation © Rawley Grau, 2019

Cover design and typesetting: Davor Pukljak | www.frontispis.hr

ISBN: 978-1-912545-25-4

This Book is part of the EU co-funded project *"Reading the Heart of Europe"*
in partnership with Beletrina Academic Press | www.beletrina.si

Co-funded by the
Creative Europe Programme
of the European Union

The European Commission support for the production of this publication does not constitute an endorsement
of the contents which reflects the views only of the authors, and the Commission cannot be held responsible
for any use which may be made of the information contained therein.

Contents

If anywhere there is an eye that is bigger than life, then its gaze must be able to embrace the entire universe, all visible and invisible worlds, both good and evil at once; people say that a person can see the whole, can glimpse the truth compressed in a single second, only at the moment of crossing between life and death. But the question remains: are all these crossings, these final seconds, also captured in the gaze of that great eye? In other words, does it only see them or does it also remember them? Does the eye ever shut and recall?

A Lullaby

1

A dull, hollow sky stretched down to the squat houses, which were wheezing shallow breaths into the damp, stifling air. These strange, colourless exhalations, rising from the dead earth and errant mists, had settled in front of the town – the *varaš* – like a mighty ghost from the past which not even children believed in any more. The secret that once lingered in these parts had again had to flee. It could be felt in the strange murmuring that hovered above the open plain. Now, at the hour of its departure, a sticky emptiness was opening. Somewhere deep down only oil stains and pillars of rock salt remained. Hidden in dense fog, which no wind would disperse for a long time, lay the last evidence that life could be any different.

The shine had faded long ago from the silver coffee spoons, and the determined clack of chessmen on chessboards, once intermingled with fervent conversations, had fallen silent. In the background of this genteel and seemingly well-mannered play of words and wit, the town lived its other, secret life. One sensed it as a devious, dire, even incurable disease that was slowing eating away at the idyllic façade. Perhaps it was only the spirit of the age, about which there had been so much discussion, but everyone agreed that the golden years they had shared were passing, the days when on the street, in coffee houses or at the cinema, the people of this small world, hidden from the world outside, would meet and greet each other as in a big communal garden.

Sadness, inexplicable melancholy and staring at dark landscape paintings and faded photographs, long solitary daydreaming and, especially, sinking into silence – these were all signs of the chronic disease that had been gaining power over the *varaš*.

At this hour, in late March, in the year 1945, all that could be heard from the cellar bars and illicit taprooms was an incomprehensible mix of half-drunken tongues struggling to keep up with the tuneless wail of violins and cracked drums. Now the only things in tune, playing with manful resolution, were the army bugles, which were summoning soldiers to the final march.

That night the story of good men and women could barely stand up to the devious wind dispassionately erasing the words on the faded monuments of the law. This mysterious force was stronger than the storms and deeper than the floods that were once talked about here. It came as a vague feeling, or a long, harrowing dream, which burrowed into people's souls even before they fell asleep or drank themselves into a stupor.

All of this was pressing down from above on this forgotten, sleepy town, tired of contrived splendour and barren grandeur, too tired perhaps even to die, as hope had died – hope in the coming of the one who will judge by the letter of the law.

The wooden roller blinds on the tall windows of the middle-class houses and shops on Horthy Street were tightly shut; somewhere deep behind these windows, beneath the cool ceilings of drawing rooms, in sitting rooms that looked out on gardens still gripped by icy dew, words were few, wrenched out like a hacking cough for which no medicine existed.

'Brandy taken with honey and bed rest – that's the only thing that helps,' people said on the street. But for timidity and especially the fear that comes from a chronic lack of will, there was no effective medicine. So the silence and the rare, awkward word uttered behind thick walls sank ever deeper into memories of earlier, better days. What was growing ever louder, and was, so to speak, already at the gates of this unwalled, sleepy *varaš*, which shook with every Pannonian breeze, only a very few saw in their sleep. It was something wild and destructive, yet at the same time liberating, like a strong home remedy for a bloody cough, which in large doses causes intoxication, madness and often even death.

The small windows, too, in the working-class and semi-farming houses, which stood in regular rows abutting long, muddy streets, were draped in thick, oft-mended curtains, which almost nobody took down, even during the day. In these low, dark little rooms, people spent entire days just sitting and waiting, the life slowly draining from their pale faces and watery eyes. For the past four years, the invisible river of time had been flowing through them, and was filled with all the hatred and despair its eddying current had picked up and carried from somewhere far away. In this peaceful, level terrain, where the river became more sluggish, where it almost came to a stop, it was slowly unloading this unbearable burden.

All of this lay on the souls of the silent, patient people who in this remote and hidden world were obediently sitting and waiting. In their humility and devotion they might well have been chosen by God himself. Devotedly they bore the senselessness of a world they knew only by hearsay, and did so for no other reason than to keep the world from collapsing on the muddy plain and falling forever into the universal abyss.

Thus had the town stood long years in isolation, gazing inwards and almost forgotten – by God, by grand politics and even by the slaughters of war. But now, as the war was approaching its denouement, an evil eye had suddenly started exchanging glances with this backwater world.

The end of the war was on the doorstep; one sensed it in the sordid peace in which the townspeople were so soundly asleep.

But every so often, from somewhere far away, from beyond the heights of Srebrni Breg, where the view opened onto the endless, rolling plain, across Hungary, Poland and all the way to the Baltic Sea, came the sound of muffled explosions.

It was not stars that were reflected on the Pannonian sea, but artillery fire. On a night such as the one that day in March, a night too dark for early spring and much too dark for the first red spring, of which there were already whispers, one might from a high balcony have seen the illuminated star of the Kremlin. But there were no high balconies here, and no one had climbed a church tower in a very long time, so everyone relied solely on rumours, half-truths, hopes and, especially, on fortune tellers, who from behind every corner were gazing into the future.

2

The muffled explosions were heard, too, by the man walking beside a road lined with poplars, which all these years had kept growing into the sky as though indifferent to the burgeoning madness in people's heads, but to him the sounds were merely the sighs of the people of Sóbota, who were still falling out of bed in their sleep, as children do the first night they sleep alone.

The man, hunched over as he trudged along the ditch beneath the poplars, next to the road from Rakičan to Sóbota, only now realized, when he heard in the distance the almost simultaneous chiming of the Catholic and Lutheran bells, that he had nearly reached his goal.

'That's Sóbota,' he murmured through cracked lips. His dry, ashen face, concealed by the rumpled, broad brim of his black hat, bore no signs of either joy or despair. His deep eyes, sunken in his bony skull, held a gaze that nothing could ever again excite. It was as if their light, coming from some inscrutable interior, had seen all the horror and beauty of this world. Now those eyes were staring, as if at rest, at the shape of the dreaming *varaš*, somewhere beyond the real world.

He leaned against a poplar, which was already sprouting its first green leaves on its long, thin branches. He hugged the tree to keep from keeling over. He was afraid of collapsing and falling asleep like Šamuel Ascher, his travelling companion, whose strength had given out in the park in Rakičan. This must have been only a little way back, no more than a hundred yards or so, but how much time, how many years had passed since then – this was impossible to know.

The slender, upright trees had kept rising from the earth even when no one was watching. The poplars would still be growing by the side of the road even when there was no one left to step into their lengthy shadows. Those endless, dark bands, which touched the very edge of the limitless plain, might one day be the only things reaching across the horizon.

Wounded and weary from travelling, the figure stood benumbed in the middle of the plain, only an arrow's shot from the town, over which the March sky was already turning red. He waited in vain for the gates of some mighty wooden tower to open. The poplars grew silently into the endless sky.

3

The dew on the old gravestones was sparkling in the morning sun. Lighter than fog and transparent as ether, the air was hung with shadows, which seemed to have just now separated from the names that remained in the gold Hebrew inscriptions. There were not many who could still read them, and even fewer who knew the law, but that morning it was as if the forgotten holy days had returned.

For it was said: Honour the holy days and you will see tomorrow as if it were today.

The sky above the Jewish cemetery had brightened. One felt the presence of souls hovering over the consecrated ground. It was still early; the town, on the other side of the railway tracks, was only now waking up, achingly, from its long doze.

In the shuffle of heavy footsteps on white gravel and the soft rustling of the poplars, the only other audible sound came from the first birds flying in small flocks across the sky. But whenever the footsteps stopped for a moment, as if the man had forgotten himself and was gazing at the faded names on the stone pillars, something else could be heard, as well. Something that was not the murmur of migratory birds beneath the blue sky or the clacking of the stiff joints of those who had just woken up. Perhaps it was a voice that had never yet been heard, although it was written that one day it would speak.

Whatever it was, Franz Schwartz heard something that morning that had long lain dormant inside him.

The light hung above the plain. The dew was slowly evaporating. The gravestones in the old cemetery were getting paler, as the last drops of moisture trickled down the black obelisks and obscured the names and dates. Gleam and glisten were now lost in sharp brightness. Franz Schwartz, fugitive and newcomer returning to his lost home, flinched at the long, shrill blast of a whistle. The ground in the cemetery trembled. He would have stood there much longer if the train, wheezing its way to the nearby station, had not disturbed him. In the distance he saw the thick cloud of smoke. It rose above the Catholic church and covered the sun over Sóbota. The refugee in the long black overcoat, which had once belonged to a soldier from God knows which army, stepped again onto the dusty road. Here, he hoped, his journey was coming to an end.

But now, when he was practically in the town, he was seized by dread. He felt that he was only at the beginning. That everything he had carried inside him over the past year, as he wandered across this bleak and alien land, had vanished in the morning dew. Everything was different here, he realized at the next whistle blast from the old locomotive, which had laboriously drawn to a stop at the small railway station. Franz Schwartz stood for a moment on the tracks he had just crossed and gazed at the station.

In the distance, the locomotive was releasing its steam, and the exhausted engine and the station buildings were swallowed in a white cloud. The whistling and rumbling of the heavy machine were enough to drown out even the bells tolling from both churches. The noise and the thunder of the bells must surely have woken every last person. Time seemed to have stopped. For an instant everything around him was still: the birds hung motionless in the air, the grass did not stir, the blood froze in his veins. Franz Schwartz now saw far behind him. In deepest darkness, images began to move.

He was watching the ordinary, everyday order of the arrival and departure of the train from Goričko, which was depositing students with books slung over their shoulders, village gentry in their best suits with large briefcases, workers in patched trousers and women with big kerchiefs on their heads and enormous straw bags in their hands. Hidden in the bags were jars of curd cheese, eggs and the occasional chicken. All of it these wives, mothers and housemaids would sell to the wealthy ladies of the *varaš* in a few brief circuits round the town.

The black-market trade had expanded greatly over the past four years. Hunger and the disintegration of the old order, both brought about by the war, had taken their toll.

Surreptitiously, at the back door, elderly gentlemen and ladies were selling small items of great value on the black market: silver, artworks, jewellery, even family heirlooms. Anything whose lack would not outwardly or too obviously compromise the visible lustre and trappings of wealth was slowly disappearing from display cabinets and from under pillows. Nothing was left on the walls but dusty frames; dust was collecting, too, in the empty, artfully decorated chests of drawers, while family photographs now stood alone on mantelpieces. Many of those who had once proudly posed in front of some respected photographer's camera lens were by now long gone. Letters arrived only rarely, or a telegraph saying that the person was missing or in prison or dead.

This forbidden exchange, this black-market commerce – which was nothing but one great sadness, a struggle for sheer survival – best portrayed the reality here. Not death, terror, incitement to violence, the recruits or the quickly suppressed Partisan resistance, but buying and selling, the clandestine barter with reputation, power and envy – that was the great local war.

It must have been nearly a year ago at this same railway station that he last saw his wife and son. They were being herded with the others by Germans in pressed uniforms and polished boots, while Hungarians in hunting jackets trotted subserviently alongside them. The train from Goričko had been whistling and wheezing in the same lazy voice it did now. As soon as the Hungarians, with exaggerated, feigned fury, had unloaded everyone from the cold, sooty carriages, the Germans very meticulously divided them up. The men were lined against the wall of the station, while the women and children were packed into Černjavič's pub, which stood on the platform. The bar was shut down for an hour. The pub's few patrons – mainly labourers, who were normally found here first thing in the morning nursing a cider or brandy, and travellers without luggage – were banished to the garden, from where they were forced to watch the scene at the station.

It was the very same blast of a steam whistle, in this half-deserted and forgotten station, or *alomaš*, as people called it, that blared forth that April day in 1944 and so deadened all their bodies that they more or less automatically, almost mechanically and with no real expression on their faces, moved towards the platform; their eyes, swollen and white, would never close again but would only stare into an emptiness filled with whistling, shouting, wailing, weeping and sobbing – they would, in other words, be guided only by sounds and voices, which became unbearably louder and louder until all that remained, above the world and in their memories, was an attenuated, monotonous, almost supernatural soundscape, filled with smoke escaping from the boiler of a superheated locomotive.

Franz Schwartz again saw them, now after long years, as he gazed at the quiet, nearly forgotten station, with only poplars beside it looking down from above and, hovering just over their pointed crowns, white cumulous clouds; he saw them, people holding tight to their sleepy children, suitcases and hastily wrapped packages, from which protruded silk-embroidered tablecloths, big down-filled pillows, fur collars and books, with oils on canvas cut from expensive frames hanging from open handbags like long loaves of fresh bread.

No one was speaking, everything was unfolding so quickly, people showing a certain inborn submissiveness and attention, which is to be expected of those who have been taught that order must always be observed. They would, of course, complain later, when they had a chance to speak to the men in charge, the highest authorities, who sit in quiet offices – no, no, now isn't the time, and anyway, what's the point of talking to these people whose uniforms aren't even of the proper rank; they look like mere workmen, carrying out explicit orders from above; you won't get anywhere with them, they're just doing their job. Of course, everything is documented, but the paperwork seems all right, in order, signed and stamped; there must have been a mistake, a big mistake, which these people certainly can't understand, let alone resolve. Now they just had to be patient, to make sure nothing in their precious luggage went missing, and they had to watch the children, who were getting restless and curious – they don't know what's happening either, but somehow it will all work out in the end.

Franz Schwartz's words had been lost forever in the unbearable thunder and groan of the old train. Even that lazy, temperamental machine must have felt something that morning. People departed without saying goodbye. They were swallowed by the fog and the steam.

The wind borne by the plain from the east was dispersing the smoke from the station and distributing it noisily among the houses. It was then that whatever hope Franz Schwartz still carried inside him collapsed. He knew that Ellsie and Izak would never again appear out of the fog. Here, for a long time to come, people would still be getting on and off trains, embracing each other and saying their fare-wells, but he would always be waiting. He alone would be walking across the tracks and watching for the train that would one day take him away, too.

As the train pulled out of the station he thought of Šamuel Ascher. The regular pounding of its wheels and the wheezing of the tired engine were coming closer and closer. The smoke that rose from the superheated boiler was now almost white as it trailed directly above the tops of the rickety carriages. The locomotive was accelerating.

Franz Schwartz continued to gaze at the monster, which was blowing its whistle louder and louder, since by now the driver had certainly seen him. And he, for his part, saw the fireman, whose black hand was gripping a small red flag and waving it at him. From the station to the cemetery, where the railway crossed the road, was less than two hundred yards, not far but still enough distance for the train to be approaching him at a hurtling speed.

Mainly, however, that minute was time enough for a decision. For a step that a short while before had seemed impossible. In that piercing whistle, which went right through his body, Franz Schwartz – shopkeeper, former proprietor of a general store, gentleman and, especially, husband – decided to take this step.

But he had promised Šamuel Ascher, who was lying somewhere in Rakičan Park, that he would get him home.

The train blew its whistle; hot, dense steam shrouded the crossing and, mixed with the dust of the road, rose into the sky. The crosses in the town cemetery and the black gravestones in the Jewish cemetery, forlorn beside the tracks, again trembled. The whistle was heard throughout the *varaš*, which was lounging with seeming indifference in the middle of the endless plain. It was as if a ram's horn had sounded, to awaken at last the souls of this sleepy town.

4

The locomotive, with its wooden carriages jumping along the tracks like crates of potatoes, was already in the middle of farmland. The terrified recruits in the first two carriages crowded around the open windows. Through the smoke and the soot, with tears in their eyes, they were looking back towards the station, as it receded to an invisible dot. In the last car, drunken officers and their adjutants, in German and Hungarian uniforms, were sitting with rifles in their hands. For several days now their generals, bewildered and lost, had been shuffling them around, carting them back and forth across the plain. They were all making plans in their hearts to flee this godforsaken place. They suspected that the train wouldn't get very far. Many of them would soon be sent back to the station on foot, the ones who already carried death inside them, only they did not know this. They were all just waiting for the moment when this hapless train would approach the Mura River. The Germans, who had begun to feel that time was running out, were desperate to cross it. The mighty wind that was driving them from the east like dry leaves would soon be here. For the others, it was by now clear that they would do better to stay. If the end was coming, it was best to wait for it here. The soldiers were counting on the train slowing down before it reached the garrisoned bridge; at that moment they would all leap through the open doors and take off in all directions across the fields. They would hide in the dead pools of the river and wait for night to come, wait even, perhaps, for the war to end. It was only the Germans who still shot at deserters, but maybe before the train reached the bridge they would be drunk on the liquor the recruits were offering them. These days nobody knew for sure who you had to be afraid of or who you had to shoot.

It was being said more and more out loud, even among ordinary soldiers, that the thunder and occasional explosions, originating somewhere in distant Russia, were getting closer and closer. Russian bullets could now reach even here. Gunfire was being heard in the Goričko forests, the Raba valley and the villages on the plain, and there had been a succession of small diversions as well, and the anxiety of the Arrow Crossists and local administrators was escalating. Partisans, it was said, had again infiltrated the region, although no one had yet seen them. But they knew they were dangerous. After all, they had ties with the Reds, who were advancing across the steppes.

A month ago, in the middle of February, Budapest had fallen. One of the Hungarian privates, a boy barely out of adolescence who was carrying a fiddle in his duffel bag, was already good and drunk, even at that early hour. He wasn't used to the strong liquor, in which he had been drowning his fear and comforting his soul. They had been drinking it for several days on end. He stood up from the wooden bench and cried out that his Budapest had turned red. The snow, which had come down in great heaps in February and covered Buda and Pest in white – he explained, gasping for breath – was now, after the invasion of the Red Army, red with blood. Blood was falling from the sky. Saying this, he took another long draught of the liquor and then spat on the floor.

'Play for us, István, play something,' his mates started shouting. The boy pulled the fiddle out of the duffel bag and, with full concentration, as if instantly sobering up, he began to play. All of them – the Sóbota recruits, the Hungarian soldiers, the train driver, the fireman – everyone knew this sad Hungarian melody. It spilled from the creaking carriages into the dewy morning, somewhere between Sóbota and Beltinci.

They sang like a chorus of condemned men whose necks had just been sliced through. The train whistled on towards Beltinci station, where a new contingent of frightened boys, with unshaven cheeks and forcibly shaven heads, were waiting.

'So where are we supposed to put them?' the train driver yelled, with a cigarette pressed between his lips and his hand on the brake. The song and the plaintive wail of the fiddle had by now reached the approaching station. But the sound was blurred and no one could say if this was a song of despair, sadness or joy.

5

At the last possible moment, Franz Schwartz stepped across the tracks. The smoke and dust had still not settled by the time the train was approaching Beltinci. Then a shot rang out. Followed by a short burst of shooting. The sudden gunfire, which pierced the deafness of the morning, could be felt all the way to the town. Franz Schwartz heard it, too, as he ran towards the Catholic church and then, gasping for breath, turned at the intersection, right next to Bajlec's house, into Church Street. He stopped for a moment opposite the Naday house, where some barrels of wine were being unloaded from a cart. That's when the echo of a second burst of gunfire reached Sóbota. The Hungarian private lay dead on the floor of the carriage, his liquor glass under his neck. The fiddle, surrounded by hobnailed boots, was still reverberating beneath the bench.

Although one of the Hitlerites yelled that they should chuck the fiddle out of the window and the fiddler with it, no one could bend down and reach it because of the crush in the carriage. For it was then that the hapless train stopped and the new herd of recruits pushed their way on.

The plain stretched in long, evenly spaced ribbons from the creaking locomotive to the horizon, and across these taut furrows, like a bow across strings, the Pannonian river slithered and weaved. The earth was ringing, groaning and in slow, muted, minor chords, receding into the universe.

Although it had been nearly a year – from the end of the previous April to late March 1945, when Franz Schwartz returned to the town – everything was the same as always. It was as if during those eleven months, when he was walking on the brink of hell, which he had previously heard only the most fervent, God-fearing Catholics talk about, nothing whatsoever had happened here. Now he could assure those virtuous, pious men and women that everything that had been preached to them out of books was true. The only thing he could not understand was why their priests would be spared all this misery. For he had seen things that perhaps would never be written in books.

The tall, two-storey houses of the local elite, with commercial spaces and workshops below and residential quarters above, were still standing peacefully in a row. Nothing had been either destroyed or renovated. The façades with their tall windows and half-drawn blinds looked down on the empty streets with a weary and rather absent, almost musing, gaze.

The boys who were wrestling with the heavy barrels, which were filled with the highly valued wines of Lendava and Filovci, took one look at the ghost and fled into the cool corridors of the Naday house, leaving the merchandise in the street.

The only change here, which the newcomer noticed at once, was the sign above the door, which said: *Mura Valley Wine Merchants – Proprietors J. Benko, A. Faflik, L. Bac.*

Franz Schwartz, proprietor of a general store, property owner and building materials wholesaler, remembered these respectable gentlemen very well. Clearly, they had done excellent business during the time he was gone. That came to him quickly, as if he had cracked open a door no one had used in a long time.

He also had no trouble recognizing the Cvetič textile factory, which looked especially dreary. From its yard you would always hear the shouts of the supervisors driving the women to work faster.

Clearly, the sewing machines were not rumbling today, devouring miles of sharp thread.

He walked on. Brumen's shop on the corner was also closed. He glanced down Court Street; it was completely empty. He hurried past the courthouse and stopped in the middle of the big, wide intersection. Large teams of horses could easily make turns here. To his left he saw the Bac Hotel, whose owner was the same gentleman mentioned on the earlier sign. Not a living soul was in sight. Even the wine barrels were still sitting abandoned in the street.

What day is it? he wondered.

Days, months, almost years – he had long ago stopped counting them. At first, the Jews who were together in the internment camp had tried at least to remember which days were Saturdays, but in the labour camps the Germans and Hungarians soon managed to erase all sense of time. During the day they were transported in dark cattle wagons from worksite to worksite, where at night they dug trenches and moats. Later, they were often abandoned to the mercy and cruelty of the Allied bombers dropping bombs left over from the raids on Budapest. Muddy and hungry, they would lie there sometimes for days on end. After each air raid, the trenches were like poorly dug graves that needed to be reopened again and again. They were suspended between sky and earth, their feet in the graves, their heads among the stars. Days and dates lost all meaning. Living corpses, repeatedly buried and exhumed, as if rising from the dead and lying down with the dead, they now observed only the phases of the moon. At night in the ditches, they would watch its waxing and waning. But the moon, too, was often obscured by clouds, smoke and mortal weariness.

In the end, it was time that remained, duration without rhythm. Time, like a long, liberating but also destructive silence after music. A silence that opens into the interior.

6

The cold, gaseous sphere hung motionless over the town. The houses, the plane trees and poplars that lined the streets, the bell towers, the man – all were left without shadow. The sharp, blinding light had painfully imprinted an image of the morning on the consciousness of Franz Schwartz. In a succession of short exposures, one after the other as if he was blinking his eyes, the pages of a large photo album were being turned inside him. He stood in the middle of the inter-section, entirely alone. He looked down Horthy Street, the former Main Street, past the rows of tall plane trees, behind which stood coffee houses, a pharmacy and shops. His eye reached all the way to Main Square, where he could see the green of the chestnut trees in front of the Hotel Dobray. He felt he could see even further, past the compact row of Jewish shops, as people called them. He knew every one of them; how could he not? His inner eye reached all the way to Lendava Road, beyond the bend on the right. The Hartner house was still standing on the corner, next to Kirbisch's pub, and on the other side of the road was Benko's meat factory and, a little further on, the synagogue. He knew all these houses and their occupants, every last one of them, all the way to Benkič's pub and the Ledava Bridge.

He had crossed that bridge countless times coming into town. In good weather he had liked riding into town on his new motorcycle, to show it off; Mr Steiner had ordered it for him from Germany. Most often, however, he had come here by train, the same train that was now somewhere in the middle of the fields, full of recruits and soldiers. For him, the train was also very convenient. His building materials business was located by the train stop in the village of Šalovci. With larger orders he had to deliver the materials to Sóbota himself, where he would then dine with the customer – maybe just goulash and coffee in one of the better pubs. It all depended on the transaction. He had suppliers and customers in both Croatia and Hungary; new business routes were also opening up for timber from Gottschee and even Italian stone. There had been a lot of construction in the region in the years before the war, especially in the town. But the villages, too, were not to be dismissed: many innkeepers knew how to attract travellers, who often enough passed through these parts headed to Szombathely, Lake Balaton and all the way to Budapest, or south to Lendava, Čakovec, and from there to Zagreb, and they made good money from it. Another route that had again been gaining importance was the one to Graz, Vienna and Bratislava; here, too, there had still been plentiful opportunities for honest trade. Modern architects, distinguished customers – it all required effort, seeking out new partnerships, and a great deal of resourcefulness. The times, to be sure, had been changing.

It was, in fact, over the Ledava Bridge that the light now came, as if it had found its way here along all the routes and on all the winds of this unhappy world. It was spilling over the streets and the houses, colouring and reviving memories. Everything was as if on a well-preserved postcard, which you keep safe even though you have no desire to look at it a second time. You guard the picture in memory of the one who mailed it to you out of love. But now he is long gone and you remain alone. The picture of the *varaš*, safely pressed between the covers of a thick book, is all you have left. The sender's smile is lost forever, and now his handwriting, too, is fading.

The fiddle was still reverberating. The soul of the Hungarian private, whose body had been tossed into a dead pool somewhere before the Veržej Bridge, would float above the plain for a long time. Its voice would be dissolving like salt until the water was as saturated as the sea. This mournful, deep singing was also heard by the man, still standing in the middle of the intersection looking somewhere far down the empty street. Or maybe by now it was a different song, the one that people here once said would never die.

At that moment a group of men came staggering out of Türk's pub, which stood on the corner. They stopped in the doorway a moment, surprised, it seemed, by the morning light. There were five, maybe six, of them. Three were carrying musical instruments, either in their hands or strapped on their shoulders. The others had their arms around each other and were leaning against the door, which the exasperated publican was doing all he could to shut. Franz Schwartz watched them from the road. They were all somehow alike. All tired and wearing long, unbuttoned and rumpled overcoats. Their eyes were on fire. It was impossible to say if they had been taking leave of each other before going off to their separate fates, or if they had stayed up all night with the musicians out of sheer happiness. Maybe they knew that the slaughter would soon be over and they would remain here forever.

'Play something, Lajči, play!' the one in the middle shouted. He was standing on the highest step supporting himself on his two mates, who were struggling to keep him on his feet. The men with the musical instruments were slowly backing away. They were watching the drunken trio and roguishly bowing to them. They had had enough, and had certainly made good money off these drunks that night. Still, they knew it wasn't over. These men would want more music. Now, with both their glasses and pockets empty, their hearts would burn all the more. They would want this music, this sad, endless music, which would ring out overhead even after they were gone. The ensemble was already in the street when one of its members, who was carrying an enormous double bass that reverberated even as he walked, looked back towards the pub. The three musicians leaned against the garden fence, as if resting, and then took off their hats. The gauntlet was thrown down. This was the men's last chance for sadness and joy. The tall one, who a moment earlier had been stumbling and leaning on his mates' shoulders, now instantly gathered his wits and was almost sober. He wriggled out of his friends' safe grip and stepped forward. Holding himself erect, he walked towards the fence. For a brief second, by a table in the pub's garden, which was anticipating the spring, he stopped and gazed past the heads of the musicians. It was then he must have seen Franz Schwartz, who was standing at the intersection looking right back at him.

Did the man recognize him? Or did that dark shape lit by the early-morning sun, in middle of the empty intersection, simply surprise and maybe frighten him, too? Or even remind him that life was not merely a nostalgic photograph in which we are captured by chance?

'Come on, Lajči, play for us!' he then said in a loud voice, too loud to be intended for them alone. 'Play something for all of us, something sad,' he added and, to the musicians' obvious approval, took off his watch and dropped it in one of their hats. The ensemble began to play.

The fiddle on the train, which was just now crossing the Mura River, had nearly stopped reverberating. But now it started up again. The train was rumbling across the iron bridge without slowing down. Everybody was still on board. That morning, nobody had fled. The only one who remained on this side of the river, in a forgotten, stagnant pool, was the dead fiddler.

7

The old porcelain sky was polished to a shine. It lay motionless above the black earth. Like a coffee cup someone had long ago turned upside down on its saucer. Perhaps this was the work of one of the many fortune tellers who read coffee grounds. Now the black sediment had covered the saucer, and high above it, in the blue of the sky, only small traces could be seen, broken signs and mysterious shapes, which only the most inspired could interpret. That morning one of these women kept glancing at the black sludge as if she was looking at the sky; then she'd merely shake her head and spit out a thick, grimy dollop of phlegm. She was sitting on the front steps of the Hotel Dobray and every so often would turn her eyes away from the witchery in her right hand and look up Main Street. There was nobody to be seen, which was a good omen. For it was best, the women said, if the person they saw in the coffee grounds was never seen by living eyes. Then, with a deep, rasping sound, she hawked up phlegm from her entire torso, so much that the child she carried inside might soon be left dry, and she spat all this life into her free hand. She squeezed and rolled the glob around in her hand a few moments, then opened it. The thing she held in her hand now slowly started to expand, like rising dough or boiling milk. At that very moment, in the empty, glazed sky, a speck appeared, or rather, a shadow the size of an eye. Now the woman fixed her eyes directly on that nearly imperceptible shadow in the sky and mumbled: 'Chicken, chicken coop, chicken eye, I see ya, I'm looking right at ya …'

Then she put the big green eye that had risen on her palm into the coffee cup, and again turned the cup upside down on the saucer. The world was reassembled; sky and earth, which had been divided, were again safe in the woman's warm hand. Only nobody knew just what that big, green, slimy eye was seeing.

In any case, in these thick, black coffee grounds lay a town that had had many names. Every ruler who had ever for a time claimed this lost and forgotten child as his own had given it a new name. It had been this way ever since the first inscriptions in the fourteenth century, when it was mentioned as *Zombotho*. A settlement on the territory of *Belmura*. In 1366, this settlement was first called a town, with the name written as *Murazumbota*. Experts agree that the town's earliest name should be ascribed a Slavic origin, but later, when the entire region between the Mura and Raba rivers came under Hungarian rule, the Hungarian designation became official. Thus in the oldest clerical records the name is preserved with the prefix *Mura*, *Murai* or *Muray*, all of which derive from the name of the river. So it was for centuries.

And so it was, too, on that Sunday in March in the year 1945, when the days of the Hungarian occupation were numbered. The child was soon to be rechristened – which could everywhere be felt – but the soul-damaged, aggrieved gentlemen in the uniforms of Hungarian officers, who were assembled that morning at the bar of the Hotel Dobray, refused to believe it. They were all staring at the telephone and drinking. They hadn't slept the night before or, indeed, for several nights in a row. Their women had been lying alone all this time in unmade, sweat-stained beds. The men, who in the street or at military headquarters conveyed an image of manliness and heartlessness, had in recent days been avoiding the staircase that led to the hotel's upper floor. Always a little drunk, sometimes very drunk, and with bloody saliva in their mouths, they were acting like boys who wanted to spend just one more night with their sweethearts but in their thoughts were already home, somewhere far away, where what awaited them was something they feared more than all the madness and bloodshed here. They knew that from now on things would never again be as they had once been.

The telephone, which had been placed in the middle of the long counter, remained silent. The soldiers and junior officers were smoking dry tobacco and knocking back glasses of spirits. Everything was gradually running out, the same way their patience was dwindling and their anxiety increasing, the same way their tobacco was running out and the fear inside them was swelling. The hotel's coffee house was in a more or less woeful condition. For the past month, virtually none of the townsfolk had set foot there. The mood was no different on the other side of the counter. The man tending the bar, the only employee left, who had stayed out of some coffee-house ethic no one now understood – Laci, the maître d'hôtel, was comporting himself like the captain of a slowly sinking ship. His cooks, cellarmen, barmen and managers had long ago fled. Laci struggled on alone, waiting tables, purchasing liquor in the middle of the night from black marketeers who mercilessly fleeced him, washing dishes and carrying drunken soldiers on his shoulders to the storeroom to sleep it off. He no longer had the strength to deliver them to the women upstairs. The only thing he truly neglected these days was the cleaning, which had never been his job, and he wasn't about to take it on now.

Cleaning, tidying up, scrubbing floors – that was his inner boundary and he couldn't cross it. So with each passing day the hotel looked more and more like the kind of seedy dive that could be found in growing numbers in cellars all around here. The only difference was that he still had the feeling that he was operating legally, that he was abiding by the ordinances and regulations which were posted on the walls. In his almost mad perseverance, even when everything was slowly going to hell, he could best be compared to the ladies upstairs lying devotedly on their filthy bed sheets. Laci and his ladies were the last mariners on board, the only remaining hope for order, lawfulness and professional ethics in the black coffee slime that was relentlessly engulfing everything.

'Get ready, men, the Secretary is coming,' said Laci the hotelier; he was the first to hear a woman's cries and the gallop of male feet descending the hotel's creaking staircase. It wasn't so long ago that gentlemen would come down these same stairs with slow, tired footsteps, from the casino that had been operating for many years on the first floor.

Laci could still recall the mornings he would wait by the door for the last of the gamblers, who left the hotel feeling relieved and with that mysterious smile on their faces. There were usually gypsies waiting for them on the doorstep, who had come here for one last dinar. These musicians performed in pubs and coffee houses around town and beyond, but in the morning they would come here, since the casino was open all night. Sometimes several bands would stand beneath the chestnuts all at the same time, all waiting, almost competing to see who could play the saddest, most heart-rending melody.

The gentlemen had always saved them a dinar or two in the hope that the musicians, with their fiddles, basses and accordions, would accompany them along the dewy streets on their way home. The gypsies, who all knew who lived where, would withdraw at just the right moment, so as not to wake the wives and children of these drunk and strangely melancholy men who had been up all night playing cards.

József Sárdy, secretary of the Office of the Special Military Tribunal, stepped through the swinging doors and surveyed his army. At Laci's warning, the men had strapped on their belts as best they could and pushed their glasses to the end of the counter, but they were unable to hide their tipsy and demoralized state. Their condition, indeed, was not unlike that of the coffee house itself. Overturned chairs were scattered about the room, a few on the tables where they'd been for days; the curtains were perforated with cigarette holes, while the floor was strewn with old newspapers, on which the soldiers would wipe their boots. Only the chandeliers, which hung high overhead, still testified to the evenings when fine gentlemen used to sit beneath them.

A bit of yellowish light, penetrating the leafy chestnuts in the courtyard, was now caught in the dusty globes of glass beneath the ceiling and painted a rainbow across the walls. Perhaps it was merely a play of light, which might possibly be interpreted as a sign that the eye looking down on them was also present, or perhaps it was some unfathomable irony, even mockery of everything happening here. But its true importance, or more specifically, its meaning, was at that moment lost on József Sárdy, secretary of the Office of the Special Military Tribunal, who in fact had not understood anything for a long time.

'You're exactly the same as those tarts, those damn whores!' he swore at the men. 'I knew this would end up as one big whorehouse. The world is sinking in black mud and all you do is wait for something to happen. Well, let me tell you, it won't be long before you're pissing blood, and not from Laci's booze either. But first the Reds will stuff our guts with maize, and then you worthless swine will see how the godless pray!'

József Sárdy, secretary of the Office of the Special Military Tribunal, didn't wait for an answer – he knew that no one here would dare say a thing to him. So now his words just bounced off the crumbling walls. In the only remaining hotel far and wide, nothing was heard but the trickle of the liquor Laci was pouring from a wicker bottle into the shot glasses. But before the last drop had fallen, there again came the sound from upstairs of a woman shouting.

'You bastard, you goddamn good-for-nothing!' Sugar Neni was screaming – that's what everybody called her. She was the main woman here. Before the war, there were almost always seven ladies upstairs, who regularly, every evening, would sit in front of the doors of three rooms, if they weren't entertaining gentlemen in the casino or coffee house. They normally sat at the same table with the fiddlers, who didn't always consider this an honour. Now, when very few men had the courage to enter this soldiers' lair, and those who did were usually smugglers, drunks or freethinkers of dubious provenance, these ladies, too, were left without company or business. Only three still slept upstairs: Sugar Neni and two orphans, who had stayed on simply because they had nowhere else to go. If they went somewhere in town, they were sure to be torn apart by the half-starved dogs of the silent, virtuous townsfolk. People here still believed that the evil that had befallen them in these terrible years was spawned from moral indecency – from indecency in general. Indeed, one had only to look down the street or, perhaps, step into one of those once respectable houses, to be firmly convinced of this. Not even fine ladies and gentlemen were what they once were. No one could hide the black crescents beneath their fingernails or the yellowed collars on their once-starched shirts. But what most struck the eye was the mud, which could be seen everywhere, as if the earth had been soiling itself these past few years.

'I'm gonna kill ya! I'm gonna shoot ya right now!' Sugar Neni shouted from the top of the stairs. And now the soldiers were truly alarmed, as if a woman's words were the only thing able to bring them to their senses, at least for a moment. And then she was downstairs, barefoot and wearing only a slip, which hung off her bony, famished body like the white flag of a vanquished army. In her hands she held, not without difficulty, an officer's light pistol pressed against her face. The rouge on her cheeks, which had been made from paprika, was dissolving in her cold tears. Her hair was damp and matted in strands, which fell behind her ears, of which the right one was missing its earring.

József Sárdy, secretary of the Office of the Special Military Tribunal, before making any other move, lowered his left hand to his belt and felt for his weapon. He knew beyond a doubt that the firearm was his; he would have recognized it in the dark, so often had he polished, displayed and of course used it. Now, as he stood for the first time on the other side of its short, thin barrel, the pistol had never seemed more beautiful to him. Although from this same distance, just two or three steps, he had killed at least a dozen people with that gun, he was not the least bit afraid. He was gazing at the pistol, but the woman, whose entire body was struggling to support its invisible weight, a weight multiplied by despair, did not warrant even a glance from him.

'Forget it, Nenika, just forget it. You can see how easily something might happen,' the hotelier Laci tried to calm her; he was still holding the wicker bottle and a full glass of spirits. But his soothing words only strengthened her determination to do something she had never believed herself capable of doing. All her life she'd been swallowing insults, hiding invisible wounds inflicted by strangers who pointed their fingers at her and gawked behind her back. No one suspected that even she sometimes felt pain. Laci, perhaps, was the only one who had ever heard her cry, but he, too, eventually had to accept that it was all part of the job. There would be new guests arriving the next day; the broken pieces had to be picked up and pitchers refilled, and if you did it all in a friendly, obliging way, with that unmistakeable hotelier's smile, so much the better for business. Once you master the ethics of the profession and abide by its principles, not even bruises hurt so much. It never really made sense to him, but he had unwittingly learned this from the Jews, of whom there had once been many here. In their shops and pubs, and even among the regular guests at his hotel, there had been those he took as a yardstick. Always precise, always obliging, always unyielding. And, especially when it came to business, slow to take offence. Money knows no feelings, although it always arouses them, feelings of every sort – Laci took this lesson to heart. Abide by this rule and you'll be all right, he had often whispered to the women, to apprentices and even to himself, whenever he found it difficult to accommodate the drunks or the whims of gentlemen who were never in any hurry to leave.

But now, he realized, wasn't the time to bring up his simple if outdated ethics. He knew he should do something, but he didn't have the strength.

8

The chicken eye hanging in the sky was gazing fixedly at the *varaš*. It was sharp and shiny, like some unknown celestial phenomenon. One felt its presence, its mysterious pull and power, its ability to suck up anything caught in its gaze.

Franz Schwartz, former shopkeeper and camp prisoner now returning home, was walking down Main Street in the shade of the mighty plane trees. After that weary company of men had gone their separate ways, he had met no one else. They had disappeared in the narrow lanes, even as the sad music, too, which the musicians had left in their hearts, inaudibly dwindled away. The only thing growing was the chicken eye in the sky. No one could say if it was swelling from the warmth of the fortune teller's hand, still cradling the coffee cup on the steps of the Hotel Dobray, or if something much greater, something fateful, was at work.

If she had not heard a woman's desperate voice coming from inside the hotel, the fortune teller would have probably kept staring at the sky a long time, but as it was, she lowered her eyes for a moment and looked up the street towards Faflik's coffee house, as if searching for new steps to move to with all her weird thoughts. That's when she spotted the stooped shape in the long, rumpled officer's overcoat, which appeared and then disappeared in the row of plane trees. The woman became agitated; from the rattle of the porcelain in her hands it was clear that this strong woman was overcome by fear. Unable to see the creature's face, which was hidden beneath the brim of an overlarge hat, she thought the shadow was moving only in her head. Everything told her that this image meant misfortune; perhaps death itself had wandered into this godforsaken town. And now that it was here, it would stay here until it took what belonged to it.

The windows were slightly open in the hotel. The wind, which had been slowly rising and whirling up the dust on the road, had without a sound almost shut them. But one of the red scorched curtains had become trapped in the casements and was hanging out of the front of the building. That was the first thing Franz Schwartz noticed when he reached the large intersection in the middle of town. He was standing on the side of the street opposite the hotel, right next to Ascher's shop. Now there was nobody on the hotel steps. The great chestnut trees, which concealed the building's main façade, began to stir. Their abundant, lush spring leaves were fluttering, and their blossoms, newly opened, flew everywhere like a flock of birds. The tiny chicken eye in the sky was swelling into an enormous storm cloud. Now for the first time Franz Schwartz, too, looked up. This low, deep, wide sky, which here had always been home to him and which he knew so well, looked menacing. Storm clouds were multiplying out of the dazzling expanse, and behind their foaming edges, the sky glowed red. Dust gusted up on Main Square, too, and disappeared like smoke down Radgona Road. It was then that in the head of Franz Schwartz, former Jewish shopkeeper and deportee, who had just now come back to the town, the sounds of a lost violin, the rumble of thunder and the muffled bang of an officer's light pistol were all mixed together. But he was unable to make any of it out.

9

It was dark in the courtyard of Ascher's house. To the newcomer's eyes, the only bright thing was the water, which lay in great puddles wherever he turned. He could still hear the raindrops aimlessly striking against the gutters and pouring through many holes onto the veranda. In the extension to the building – the residential part, with two large rooms and a kitchen in the middle – a dim light was burning. In the main part of the building, with the shop, which faced the Hotel Dobray, nothing could be seen. Blackness hung beneath the long eaves, as if night had wrapped itself in cobwebs to keep the stray cats from ripping it apart.

This was the home of Šamuel Ascher, who was lying somewhere on the Count's land in Rakičan Park. Franz Schwartz had earlier been standing behind a corner of the building, hidden from the eyes of the rare passer-by; he was afraid because he did not yet know who he could show himself to. He knew only what he and Šamuel had heard on their travels: that the war would soon be over. Everybody was saying it was just a matter of days, ten at the most; that was all the victorious Red Army would need to rout the Germans and the Arrow Cross from Hungary and penetrate the heartland of the defeated Reich. People who in the evenings had at their disposal a contraband or confiscated radio also knew that the world had already been divided anew, that in the fashionable setting of Yalta, the Big Three had drawn a line in chalk. Europe, still bleeding, was chopped into two halves, as if the elder brothers, after the death of the father, had each staked his own claim. But clearly, just as sisters and younger brothers tend to be forgotten on such occasions, so, too, it had been forgotten that, for some time now, Europe had consisted of more than just two or three parts.

A light must have come on somewhere. The water in the large puddles, which a little earlier had merely been shimmering, was now lit up. He could distinctly see the last raindrops falling into the black lakes. It was nearly impossible to get to the extension without crossing through water. And he could feel his last strength leaving him. The world seemed to be drowning. He was afraid to take a step, to stride across the courtyard through the puddles and find somewhere he could sit down for a moment and shut his aching eyes. Blind, muddy eyes were staring at him. And there was a hissing in his ears – the rain, pounding somewhere in the distance, was burrowing into his consciousness. He was giving in, sinking. Like a well-trained animal, he lifted his arms high into the air and dropped his head towards the ground. Again he was a captive, disinherited and humbled. He walked as if through water. He was still fully conscious and knew there was no one giving him orders or chasing him or threatening him, but the voice echoing somewhere inside his head was stronger and he could no longer resist it. Something was mightier than any will of his own, as if it was grafted into his bones. Franz Schwartz, camp prisoner, Jew, former wholesaler, hands raised in the air, was sloshing, splashing and trudging through the puddles like a sleepwalking child.

On his weary, ravaged, bony face, covered in a thin, bristly beard, there appeared the barely perceptible outline of a smile. The corners of his mouth were extended and a bloody, swollen tongue was visible between his broken teeth. Whatever his watery eyes then saw, as they widened and opened into the night, he would probably never remember, but that mysterious gleam, which flickered and melted in his eyes, as if in those black lakes – this, certainly, must have somewhere remained.

He dragged himself over to a wall and lay down in the darkest corner of the courtyard. He was used to this watchful hovering in semi-sleep. His body, wrapped in damp, foul-smelling rags, quivered and winced at every noise that came out of the darkness. Although he was trying to rest his eyes, they kept opening, peering into the void lurking inside him. He was walking, was running in his semi-sleep; he could feel his feet sinking in the sodden earth or pounding painfully against the macadamized road, which stretched to infinity. More and more, it seemed, someone else was living inside him, someone he would never know. His body was inhabited by a different consciousness, which kept eluding him, slipping away and always hiding from him. At first it had come merely as a beautiful thought, an illusion that helped him escape reality. When things were at their worst and he felt he might go mad or die, he would cling to the beautiful thought and run far away. Thus hours, days, would go by while he lived as if he had abandoned his body. He would be digging ditches in the muddy snow, burying the dead, starving and marching and sleeping on bunks with people whose faces he never saw and whose names he never learned – but that was only where his empty, emaciated, battered body was living. He himself, meanwhile, would be somewhere else, following the beautiful thought, which protected him and led him down other roads, far from reality and even further from his memories.

But now that he was, as it were, outside, far away from all that and very close to home, he sensed that the illusion, the beautiful thought, had led him astray, almost too far astray. Now, as he was genuinely trying to fall asleep, he was again on the road. He struggled against the beautiful thought and especially against that music, the seductive sound of a violin, inviting him to leave one last time, to go away and vanish completely.

10

His eyes twitched and opened wide into the darkness at a rustling sound, very close by, which came from the white gravel that covered the little path around the building. He recognized this sound from the years before the war, when he himself had walked over this gravel to see the younger Ascher on social or business visits. The path was always carefully raked and clean. There were never any leaves or gaps, which was surprising, considering how many people came and went here every day.

He was lying next to the wall, absolutely still and covered to his ears by the damp army overcoat, with his hat beneath his head. He first made out the sharp step of a man, who, he was sure, was wearing boots. But there was another step, too, lighter and shorter, woven into the sound. From the way it came precisely mid-stride with the sharper, longer step, he was sure that two people were walking side by side. They were walking without hesitation, as if they were familiar with the path and knew where they were going. Although at first he was terrified, convinced that it was him they were looking for, his anxiety soon subsided: the two people, he was now sure, were a woman and a man, who were walking on their own path with their thoughts somewhere else. They were driven, he felt, by something that had nothing to do with him or the world, which was still enveloped in darkness.

By the time they hurried past, even though they were very close, he was completely calm, as if it was an earlier time, when people would pass each other on this well-tended path with pure thoughts, concerned only for business and the welfare of their families. In their footsteps, too, there had been no greed, fear or arrogance, but only concern, focus and full concentration on life. In the step and bearing of these men in simple black suits and the obligatory head covering, usually a hat, who walked on the gravel without leaving marks or gaps, even if they were shuffling along in light shoes and the sound could be heard as far as the street, there was something that made one think of chosenness, consecration or simply total devotion. Here, in this small Pannonian *varaš*, in the middle of nowhere, far from everything, people would ask themselves: devotion to what – to God or business?

A bell chimed midnight – it was the same small bell in the Lutheran church that had long ago imprinted itself on his body. Whenever it chimed, he would glance at his tiny pocket watch and reset it. The clock on this church had always been considered precise. The local elite set their watches by it. Labourers and small tradesmen worked to its rhythm, even if the great majority of them were Catholics and, one might say, adhered to a different reckoning of time. Nonetheless, everyone agreed that the somewhat newer and more modern German mechanism installed in the Lutheran clock was trustworthy. The Protestant ethic, in its shopkeeperly and tradesmanlike manner, as expressed particularly in the qualities of industriousness and precision, had spread unconsciously and persistently to the life of the local middle class. It was visible in the way you comported yourself and the people with whom you played cards or chess. The vocabulary of humility, absolution and even piety, as taught by the Catholics, had been pushed to the margins, far removed from coffee-house conversations and expelled from the hearts of the ladies of town. All the high-flown rhetoric that had captured the souls of intellectuals, small industrialists, tradesmen and the eternally overlooked artists had now become the only possible politics. With its precision, mechanical consistency and inhuman persistence, that dubious, mendacious spirit known as modern times had possessed the minds of these poor, foolish people.

Then, a single swing, a single stroke later, the bell rang out in the Catholic church, too. The difference, of course, was insignificant, negligible in fact, but for the town, which had been half asleep for decades, here amid the endless fields, forgotten by politics and, for many, by God himself, that difference was suddenly important, even fateful.

But maybe midnight had not struck, maybe the clocks had not even moved since they had been deported, exiled from a world that seemed ever less real to him. It could all be a dream, a spell, sorcery performed by old witches and wizards with hands forged from mud. He had heard it said that if you had a heart made of ashes you could trick people, persuade them that the world was a desolate land of pain and suffering, where only evil prospered.

For as it is written: earth to earth, ashes to ashes. And now, for the first time he asked himself: Would the sorcery ever end? Was the moment of awakening at hand?

He pondered these things as he lay there alone and abandoned, with that thought which he would never be able to express.

11

He saw him when he stepped into the light. He was wearing a big white shirt, loose over unbuttoned trousers, and clutched a pair of high boots in his left hand, and an overcoat of soft leather hung from his shoulders.

Moist breezes, dissolving in the milky morning, settled in the courtyard. In the distance one could hear dogs barking and the neighing of weary horses, as if the animals were tugging at heavy chains. At the first muffled bang, the man sat down on the doorstep and hastily started putting himself in order. He pulled his narrow boots on over his trousers, and knocked his heels a few times firmly against the ground. Although there was no echo, only that muffled bang from a rifle still hanging in the air, this pounding of human feet conveyed a certain resolve, maybe even vengeance, which was impossible for him to conceal. It was then that the sole person observing him noticed something else the man could not conceal, not from anyone – the entirely human, congenital deformity of his body. Namely, he was a hunchback, which Franz Schwartz noticed now as the man tried to straighten up. Under the long, leather over-coat, which was clearly too big for him, his condition was all the more evident. The man leaned against the wall and lit a cigarette. He took quick drags and puffed out thin clouds of smoke. He was enjoying this cigarette as if it was his last.

Even before he dropped the cigarette in the mud and crushed it beneath his heel, he rapped nervously on the window, but no one responded.

He's waiting for her and they don't have much time, Franz Schwartz said to himself. Only now did he recall the two people who had spent the night on the other side of the wall. He had nearly forgotten that he wasn't the only guest at Ascher's house. In his groggy, aching head, still suspended somewhere between sky and earth as if it was not attached to his battered body, fear was the only thing nagging him now. He knew he had to find a hiding place as soon as possible, even before that peculiar couple left the house – whether they had come here out of a purely human passion or carried within themselves some entirely different message, he didn't know. They may have seemed quite innocent last night (as much as he could judge, of course), but now everything had changed.

'Give me my gun! I'm going!' the man said sharply, again rapping nervously on the windows.

'So go!' he heard a voice say firmly. 'And take your pistol, I'm not keeping it from you.'

'Damn whore, I'll teach you to coddle guns,' the man replied and ran back inside. Franz Schwartz now seized his chance and with great difficulty dragged himself away from the building. He was already expecting the man to come around the corner and discover him when his eyes fell on a summer house standing some ten yards away.

In better days it had always been freshly whitewashed. It stood in the shade of a huge plane tree, one of those that had been planted when they were putting in the trees along Main Street, by which he had arrived here. It was in the summer house – which in winter was glazed and filled with plants that spent the cold months there, while in summer people would sit in it late into the night by the light of a paraffin lamp – it was here, then, in this pavilion where Franz Schwartz now sought shelter, that the elder Ascher would usually bring his most demanding or most valued customers, usually bankers and wholesalers, as well as those who owed him money, and it was here, at the same round table beneath which he was now lying, that they would negotiate a settlement on the debt or arrange some big Sóbota business deal. It all came back to him clearly once he had hidden himself again. Now he was nothing but ears, listening to every movement or possible word that might tell him if he should be afraid of those two or if he could trust them – maybe they could even get him back to Rakičan, where Šamuel Ascher still lay, the man in whose house all of this was happening. They were obviously very much at home here: they had known exactly where the path was in the dark and when he arrived there had been a light burning faintly in the windows, which they, most likely, had left on – but he couldn't remember them from anywhere, and he knew almost everyone who used to come here, since he, too, had been a regular visitor. So those two people, and maybe there were more inside, must have come later, after all the Jews had been deported from town.

The house had been empty; it stood on a corner of the town's main intersection, opposite the only hotel in which the last Hungarian soldiers were now struggling on, held together by nothing but the mad persistence of József Sárdy, secretary of the Office of the Special Military Tribunal. Precisely because it was so visible, and was Jewish, too (as people said here), which meant that the owners were certainly dead, their bodies in a shallow grave somewhere in the depths of the Pannonian plain, in Hungary or Poland, maybe where no living person would ever find them again – for precisely these reasons, this house was the perfect place for people to visit from time to time, or even to secretly occupy; so concluded the man who was shivering on a damp floor littered with leaves and rubbish in a ramshackle summer house.

12

Across the street, at the filthy, rundown Hotel Dobray, the red curtain was still hanging out of the window. In the morning calm, when there was no one yet to be seen and only shadows were trailing down the soft, well-soaked streets, the curtain looked like a banner for the dead which some drunks must have dropped before collapsing in pools of booze. The soldiers, who were lying intoxicated on chairs and tables, did not actually know any more to whose army they belonged. They were now pretending to defend the last remaining fort in a senseless world, in a town that had been isolated all these years, playing at its own war, on land that belonged to nobody knew who. For decades, governments and armies had come and gone in turn, each with its own law in its own language, which sought to convince people that it alone was the true and proper law. So it was that in this little *varaš* people spoke and wrote for a long time in Hungarian, and then, again, in Prekmurian, which in a way was a mixture of all these languages. Many swore oaths in German, Serbian and even Czech; nor should one forget that Romany was spoken here, and Hebrew, of course, and in the year before the war many had started writing in Slovene, which was said to be the only proper language for everyone, on either side of the Mura.

Now, for a second time, war had rocked this marvellous chicken coop, where wild and domestic fowl alike crowded beneath the same rickety, leaky roof. And it was in this squalid, crappy hen's nest, as József Sárdy, secretary of the Office of the Special Military Tribunal, had recently taken to saying, that they were all going to croak. That same secretary, left without the army and tribunal in whose name he made decisions, now realized that he would have to take things into his own hands. He had introduced a few drastic measures the previous afternoon and had been refining them throughout the long night.

'Everyone to arms!' he ordered, now that the pointless gunfire with the woman had somehow ended. At the thought of his woman, that devoted creature Sugar Neni, who alone had truly remained by their side in this senseless war, he felt, perhaps for the only time, real and genuine pain. *Not even she is completely mine*, it dawned on him. *Nothing in this world is mine.* Just like these soldiers and this crappy town, which no one gives a damn about and never did, this woman, too, was not his. *Nothing is mine.* He had never been able to admit that apart from that pompous title – Secretary of the Office of the Special Military Tribunal – nothing was actually his. It was only when he called those debauched and drunken soldiers to arms, which they had probably forgotten how to use, and with his own hands herded each of them to an open window, to gaze out on the empty streets, which were now being washed in a slow rain – only then did he feel that it would have been better, would have been only right, if the woman had shot him, or at least wounded him. That would have been his only actual bleeding wound, something that might outweigh all the senseless waiting he was doing in this chicken coop. But the shot from his little gun had gone into a wall somewhere.

And everyone whose head I've ever blown off will go on staring at me from that other world – a world he couldn't name even though he was seeing it more and more often. It had to exist somewhere, for he heard all those dead men calling to him, reminding him, but mainly they were gawping at him with their pale, vacant eyes.

13

The army of József Sárdy, secretary of the Office of the Special Military Tribunal, assumed their positions one last time – which they all very well knew. Private Kolosváry, however, a man who had somehow managed to preserve his common sense and, more importantly, a particle of clear-headedness, or it might have been the voice of a conscience not utterly ruined by Laci's booze, that *palinka* – in any case, the soldier now felt a serious urge to quit, to step away and simply lay down his weapon; he was almost ready to desert, even at the price of a bullet in the head from the very pistol his commanding officer had been brooding over a little while earlier.

Kolosváry was crouching by the wall, beneath the last of the long row of tall, wide-open windows in the coffee house. From here the view looked out on a clear expanse, in which Main Square stood encircled by a broad, muddy cartway. To the right, a row of abandoned Jewish shops abutted the sodden thoroughfare, and somewhere in the middle, set back from the road, the steeple of the Lutheran church was jutting into the sky; a little further on, Main Street turned into Lendava Road. This, presumably, was the direction from which the thing they all feared would come.

More and more rumours, intimations, conjectures and prophecies were circulating, as well as visions and dreams, from both the sick and the seemingly well, which rivalled each other in the horror, detail and strength of their description of what was coming from far away, from the deepest, darkest plains, where the sun only rarely shone. Fear was always foremost in these images – fear of the devil, godlessness, chaos, debauchery, unbridled lust, alcohol, looting, the burning of money and the rejection of every sort of law, whether earthly or heavenly.

The sleepy and still intoxicated soldiers set their rifles on the windowsills and waited half-dozing with flushed faces. Their watery gazes were lost in the distance. The only thing constantly before their eyes were the tall chestnuts in the hotel's garden, and it was these they held in their crosshairs. The mighty, silent trees had just begun to put forth leaves, and later, towards evening, when the soldiers would be hungry and thirsty, when their hearts would yearn for some pungent liquid to rinse out their smoky lungs, that is, even before the sun had set on the endless plain, they would start to believe they could hear the leaves growing.

'Shoot at anyone who approaches the garden. Don't let them step into the shadow of those chestnuts,' József Sárdy concluded his orders as he backed away towards the swinging doors that led upstairs. As his sweaty palm was feeling behind him for the way out, he cast a glance one more time over the lair he was hastily abandoning. In the months he had lived here, he had somehow grown fond of it all, though he would never admit it. Now, as he gazed on the wreckage both outside and within, he was almost sad. He remembered the first day he entered this damned hotel, as he had recently been calling it.

It had been just a few days after Horthy's capitulation and the seizure of power in Budapest by the Hungarian fascists. The new government of Ferenc Szálasi and his Arrow Cross Party were calling openly for continuing the war alongside the German occupiers, mainly out of fear of the Red Army, which was surging from the east like an unstoppable flood, scattering, destroying and obliterating whatever its terrible waters touched. Everyone knew that this force, which in the stories people were telling was endowed with an almost supernatural power, needed merely a favourable wind before it ploughed across the plain and engulfed the entire wounded Reich, Hungary with it. In March 1944, the only question was the price they would pay to let the Russians flay them – such were the thoughts in those days of the young intern at the military tribunal in Budapest. After the coup and the capitulation, when the home-grown fascists came to power and Hungary was annexed to the Reich, the intern deemed it wise to accept a promotion and leave Budapest, to go somewhere far away, to a province he had never heard of, to a town he could barely find on the map. This pocket of land between the Mura and Raba rivers, at the far edge of his country, seemed a remote and safe enough place to hide and await a possible turnaround – were that, by some strange divine plan, ever to happen. But he did not believe in such a plan, even if he thought the idea itself rather credible – for why would God allow the communists, the sworn enemies of Christ, to destroy them? This, of course, was nothing but a supposition that people were deliberating in the coffee houses of Budapest, as they dreamed of a great Pannonian homeland in which horses grazed and poets wrote great Hungarian poetry, worthy of the former monarchy.

14

That boundless silence and space, where sky and earth bleed into each other and an invisible line makes an arc in the distance, like the momentary gleam of a border no one has yet drawn but which the dead are smuggling themselves across – it was there that something that morning shifted. It was as if an old warship, returning from its final battle, was trapped in a calm. The masts were broken and the tattered sails, hanging over the sides of the weary ship, were soaking in the motionless sea, which was washing the blood off the rotting ropes. The ship's men, those shattered, sleepy mariners, had been propped motionless in their cramped positions for what seemed an eternity, staring vacantly through their gunports at that invisible border thickening in their desperate hearts. Overhead, high above everything, hung the motionless sun, which spilled out across a childishly clear and innocent sky. This blue sky and this quietness were all that remained to excite the souls of those who would one day open their eyes.

The ship, becalmed in the middle of the flat sea, was sinking. Now there was no longer any expectation of a saving wind that might fill the sails and propel the ship out of this dead calm – everybody understood this more and more, as silently and without expression they toasted each other's health. The *palinka* that Laci the hotelier kept pouring in their glasses was these mariners' last hope. They drank and followed the orders of their captain, who somewhere upstairs, above their empty heads, was himself lying motionless on top of his woman.

Maybe the only thing they could still hear – or maybe they just imagined it, like the words the dead can supposedly hear in those few hours before the soul at last departs the body, this indifferent nature, and smuggles itself across the border we carry inside us – the only thing they had heard that night was the distant neighing of wild horses, who were now already grazing in the windless calm of the morning.

Horses beyond count were grazing peacefully in the middle of Main Square. All those strong black, white and brown animal bodies were tugging indifferently at the first spring grass, just a stone's throw from the Hotel Dobray. And truly, these bone-weary, inebriated soldiers could no longer distinguish mirage from reality. Kolosváry had once enjoyed reading adventure novels, and he had even been at sea, unlike his comrades, who had seen only Lake Balaton and never the 'big water', as they called it, so he was in a way acquainted with, or was at least trying to call to mind, the feeling – that feeling – when you are surrounded by sea and held in the grip of a calm. He could almost describe the anxiety, even the despair, of those who wait idly for days, or weeks, lost in the endless blue. One by one, they were all succumbing to that strange, suppressed fear of the image that lies in every person: the image or mirage or maybe just illusion, that you are looking death in the eye and neither die nor go mad.

But who knows for sure what it's like to be dead or mad, Private Kolosváry had been thinking that night as he crouched half-dazed by the open window in the Hotel Dobray, carving pictures of horses into the floral wallpaper with his rusty, blunt bayonet. He had begun by carving one of the horses he used to ride on the grasslands of Hungary, before this accursed war caught up with him and sent him to do his duty in this godforsaken town, where after all this time he still understood nothing, not even who these people were, all these fine gentlemen and ladies who couldn't decide whether or not they were Hungarians.

For although they spoke Hungarian and were full of praise for the Crown of St Stephen and for Budapest manners, which in fact they esteemed mainly from hearsay, even he, a simple soldier, who thought mostly about the freedom he was still breathing on the grasslands – even he had understood that these people were different, and now he was convinced of it, no matter what airs they put on or how high and mighty they acted; somewhere in the background, behind those well-studied words, something very different lay in their hearts, but they refused to acknowledge it.

He saw the fuss they made of József Sárdy, who wasn't the least bit better than this debauched army of his.

'All they care about is money,' Kolosváry mumbled as he pressed the dull point of his bayonet even harder into the wall.

'What'd you say? What money? Can't you see they're just grazing?' Géza, leaning at the next window, was slurring his words. Ever since the orders were given, he hadn't lowered his eye from the scope of his rifle. Géza was the most obedient but also the most terrified soldier of them all, so he was all the more courageously arming himself with *palinka*. There were always problems when he was on guard duty, and shooting was almost a certainty, so that even Laci the waiter had had to intervene with the soldier's superiors, because in his zeal, fear or drunkenness (God only knew which), he would often fire at guests who left the coffee house at night 'to get some air', as Laci said, although it was usually to have a piss or puke.

'Grazing, right; they're grazing their little fillies, and their warm arses, too,' Kolosváry replied, completely absorbed in his carvings, which by morning had covered the wall beneath the window, through which cold, dense mists were stealing into the soldiers' creaking bones.

15

He felt a cold, bony hand on his naked back. Before opening his eyes, which were buried in the damp hair of a woman, he tried to count. The bell in the Lutheran church was chiming, which in all these months he had never heard. The ringing was still echoing when that hand returned. It was somewhere below the back of his neck, as if someone had placed a heavy slab of marble on top of him which was pressing him against that silent female body. A chill such as he had never experienced, as if it was not of this world, as if something without shape or name was shining more intensely than the sun, this strange chill, neither pleasant nor alien, was pressing down on him with ever greater force. The body beneath him was suffocating, but still it did not move, did not even wake up. Wherever their insensate flesh was touching, as if they were clasped in a vice-like grip or at the height of sweetest bliss, which in fact had never occurred between them, there were puddles of cold, odourless water.

József opened his eyes when the feeling he couldn't name became unbearable. His head was flooded with a horrible white stain – it was like sinking in quicklime – and at the same moment he realized that somewhere his lost conscience was trying to make itself heard. It was like the time when, in some entranceway in Budapest, when he was still just a child, he first trampled a nest of birds. And now he again heard that unbearable chirping, the straining of tiny throats, which had diminished with every blow of his heel. Afterwards, feeling completely lost yet also giddy with power, he had run towards the tall front doors. He wanted to get away as quickly as possible, to hide in his mother's kitchen, but the doors were stuck. For a few seconds he had screamed as if he was being chased by death, of which he knew only what he had learned from the scary stories recounted by the older boys in the courtyard. They had told him: 'A person who kills isn't afraid of death.' Then, suddenly, he had come to his senses and was instantly calm. He was sitting on the damp, grimy floor. The entranceway was dark and full of silence.

József lifted himself off the billiard table, where he had been lying in an embrace with a woman who for him had no name, and walked barefoot to the small balcony. It was only when he was outside that he put the woman's silk dressing gown on his naked body; it did not even reach his knees. It was dark outside, as dark as that entranceway had been, which was still in his head. Nothing was moving; only somewhere in the distance, beyond the land that, like a black, ravenous sea, was eating into the houses on the far edge of town, there were flashes and muffled explosions from artillery fire.

It was now that József Sárdy, secretary of the Office of the Special Military Tribunal, thought of death. He knew it was close; he felt it like an invisible shadow clinging to his body with a cold hand.

He succumbed to reveries entirely unrelated to his present life. But still, he asked himself, where have those years gone when he was learning to survive on the streets of Budapest? It's not proper, it suddenly occurred to him, for an officer whom fate has appointed to lead the final battle but who in fact makes no real decisions since all the deciding is done by others, which is how it's always been in this phoney life of his – it's not proper for such an officer to indulge his memories. And again he thought: I can't walk away now; some higher necessity has appointed me to show for at least once in my life what I'm made of, and if death is the only way out, then that is what I'll choose; it's the only thing those lost boys from my street will appreciate, who are now probably hiding in some damp, dark entranceway taking their rage out on birds, if there are any birds left in Budapest.

József no longer believed that killing could save you from death, but he did believe that, for a soldier, it was the only way to fight it.

16

In the tall windows of the Hotel Dobray, which looked out on Main Square, rifles were still pointing into the night. Somewhere deep inside, a paraffin lamp was glowing. Silence lay all around, disturbed only by the relentless scratching beneath one of the windows, as if the hotel was infested with termites.

Private Kolosváry had a little earlier, at the ringing of the church bell, woken out of a brief dream. Making no attempt to shake off the images galloping through his exhausted consciousness, and so for a few moments incapable of determining if he was still dreaming or if this was just a hallucination, he grabbed the bayonet hanging from his belt and started carving horses into the wall. He was still bringing the first horse to life when he spotted a second horse next to it, and then a third, and so on until morning, when an entire herd was standing in front of him – bridled, wild, saddled, unshod; military horses, draught horses, peasant horses, noble horses, gypsy horses.

For József, standing above on the balcony in a woman's dressing gown, that faint but relentless scratching, caused by he didn't know what, made his skin crawl. The ship he commanded was slowly falling apart. He felt it being gnawed at from the inside by despondency and despair. He only hoped it would hold out until morning and the commencement of the final battle. He suspected that they had long been under siege, although nobody had told them this. In every house he saw the enemy, who during this long night must be breeding like rabbits. He had not for a long time had a single enemy here, nor in all these months had he seen any genuine danger, but now he was convinced that everybody was watching him.

They had surely occupied even that abandoned Jewish building, he said to himself as he looked at Ascher's shop, which stood forlorn on the other side of the street.

Now, however, he was no longer afraid of any living thing, and wasn't about to surrender to anybody. But the thing that lay inside him, which sounded like singing birds – this was growing, and becoming truly unbearable. Not death but something else, something he would soon have to confront, was making him afraid.

He surveyed the sleeping town beneath him, which appeared to have gone to its final rest. He, too, felt as if he was dreaming – standing bootless on this balcony in a woman's dressing gown and entirely somewhere else in his thoughts. He felt as if he was still just a traveller here, someone who had stopped in this hotel for a single night. Yet he had never actually travelled anywhere. He now imagined just how different his life would be if he had never accepted – although he had in fact requested it – that transfer to this invisible, forgotten and, for him, now long-lost world, on the very edge of his homeland. Of course, his youth was still buried somewhere inside him, but of that only ashes remained. He had known back then that he might never travel, might never sleep in modest hotels and treat himself to a night with a woman, or play billiards with a foreigner in a foreign city.

József now had nothing left but the lie; he thought of Budapest, now in flames, and remembered the day he arrived in this place, and especially the view when he first stood on this balcony, as if this was how he might change his life.

It was March 28, 1944 – just shy of a year earlier – when József Sárdy endorsed the final solution, which had been talked about so much that month at the office, although none of the junior officials, including of course himself, who was still new, understood the full meaning of those words.

It had started months before he arrived. Everyone knew that Admiral Nikolaus von Horthy could not keep steering this ship through fog and mud much longer. The Hungarian state and its imaginary kingdom without a crown had run aground long before Hitler became impatient, pressing it to take a more aggressive role in the war and, especially, to start seriously implementing the final solution – since of all the puppet regimes, Hungary alone had done nothing in this regard; even worse, the number of Jewish fugitives in the country had actually risen during this period. At the same time, it was an irrefutable fact and not just the admiral's delusion, a mirage in the fog, that actual storms and red clouds (as Admiral Horthy saw them in his delirious dreams) were amassing on the borders of this cartoon kingdom. The Russians had already set sail towards his invisible fleet.

And so, on March 19, as the admiral in his white uniform looked out from his pier across the dark and muddy sea (just as József, his unfortunate mariner, was doing now) two German divisions marched into Hungary. With them came Adolf Eichmann, the expert on Jewish evacuation and deportation, a man whom the young intern at the Military Tribunal in Budapest was destined to soon meet.

This country, which still dreamed of some ideal fascist order; which was governed by an admiral without a fleet, who was surrounded by make-believe petit bourgeois aristocrats; which worshipped the radiance of the Crown of St Stephen and was drunk on great melancholy, on the kind of music which, to be honest, only gypsies can elicit – this Hungary, then, which over the past several years had been incapable of making any decision, any gesture that might reveal its true face, had now, overnight, adopted drastic measures. On March 28, a Special Military Tribunal was proclaimed across the whole of the country.

He would never forget that day. He was young; he might still have travelled back then, he thought, but he was also entirely without prospects, poor and, above all, not ambitious enough to find his way through corridors and offices and up twisting staircases to some higher floor, where, perhaps, the view would look out across the plain. It was then that he was suddenly presented with a chance to free himself, at least for a time, from the dead birds he was hearing more and more often. Basically, he wanted to get out, far from the streets on the edge of town, the airless entranceways, his mother's bedroom and into the light, as he said, as he heard people in coffee houses say.

So he accepted the position of secretary of the Special Military Tribunal, a job no intelligent person had applied for. He was sure he would be something big, though what exactly he was unable to explain to his mother. Now, all he thought of was leaving. Back then he may even have thought of travelling – the cheap hotels, the women he had never had, the billiard games, which his new rank would now make possible.

This night, which was sinking ever deeper, as if some invisible river was claiming its own, was gradually coming to an end. Nowhere was there any sign, any clue, to give him even the false hope that night might follow night. Now it would be better, indeed, to wait for a night in which he could hide, maybe even run away, somewhere far away, instead of welcoming the day, when the sun makes every atrocity instantly known and reveals your fresh shallow grave.

Everyone here could feel that what had long been in the air would soon have to happen. Violence, rage and lust for revenge had long, too long perhaps, been kept hidden, because some still believed that personal interest, vanity and of course big business, which had flourished in this town for years, took priority over everything else, even human misery, suffering and death. Hard as it was to understand, this had for many decades been the reality here, a reality protected by a handful of petit bourgeois gentlemen, who, certainly, were now no longer able to sleep.

Now, for everyone, bells were starting to toll; voices and scrapings were being heard in the rafters, and under beds and even in people's bones, as if ghosts were summoning them, ghosts no clergyman would ever be able to banish with words alone.

17

The woman, who for him was nameless, still lay motionless on the billiard table. Her naked bony body had been rapidly wasting away in recent months, as if she was silently, almost imperceptibly and painlessly, being consumed by disease – but on the once green and well-maintained table, which was used exclusively by the local elite, it looked rather exalted, almost unapproachable. Now as József came up to her (and she was the only person allowed to call him that), chilled to the bone and almost boyishly afraid, looking as if for the first time at this woman who lay devotedly in front of him, he was almost sad. He peered into her tranquil face, framed by long brown hair, loose and damp with sweat, spreading across the green baize, which thousands of greasy fingers had touched.

He sensed the peace that lay somewhere deep behind her closed eyes. He leaned closer, as if trying to remember the colour of her eyes, into which he had never gazed. Her breath was thin but warm, although her body was strangely cool. He could feel her, but he was afraid to touch her lest she wake up. At that moment it struck him: they were closer to each other than he had ever dared admit. There was something about this woman that bound them together.

This feeling of closeness, of total devotion surpassing all else, was unknown to him.

He peered into that pale, still, tranquil face, just as he had back then, in the Jewish Library in Budapest, which he had never heard of before. He had already been promoted to secretary of the Special Military Tribunal. He was given a modest office on the first floor, albeit in the courthouse annexe, and had his own desk, a metal map chest and a telephone, which he thought particularly grand. He had stopped going home. He would stay in his office until dark, when the night guards chased him out – to them he was still a nobody. Then he would spend the evenings on the streets of Budapest; now, whenever he thought of home, it was actually only those few days that he missed, when he could almost taste freedom. At first he just strolled through the centre of the capital late into the night, next he was having drinks with disenchanted gentlemen, and ladies who hid their charms in tiny purses, and soon he was buying rounds for the bohemians and gypsies who played music on the floating platforms. All of them together were swaying on the waves of the Danube, and all of them, along with the city, the country and the world, were drowning in a sadness they alone could understand.

It was only a few days later, when he was starting to feel bored and couldn't wait for night to come, that the telephone first rang. There was no greeting at the other end and no name was given; he was told only that he had to report at once to the Jewish Library. 'Yes,' he said and spruced himself up as best he could, strapped on his belt, and looked at his pocket mirror. He almost didn't recognize himself. He said only: 'Secretary of the Special Military Tribunal', as if he had forgotten his own name.

When he left the courthouse annexe, he wondered if it was actually him they had meant to call and also, of course, where exactly he needed to report to.

He asked in a few places, but everyone just turned away. Then he offered money, but no one wanted to take it. He was starting to feel that he might be late, and was seriously worried it would mean the end of his brand new job and that the floating platforms would float away forever.

Maybe it was closeness – which alone is able to bind people into a genuine human community, and which, when we are able to profess closeness and love and pain, fundamentally defines us and, in essence, separates us from the mysterious world of nature – so maybe it was this closeness, which was never talked about in those days, that was dying then.

Death, which for a long time stood behind every house, every dream, had now crept soundlessly, like a shadow, into this forgotten *varaš*. Nobody here could speak; it was as if they had no words to express the emptiness that lay in those sealed and boarded-up houses on Main Street.

Nearly a year had passed since the Germans and their Hungarian adjutants drove all the Jews out of town in a single April night. Their houses and shops with the tall roller blinds were looted and left to this lost people, who, it was said, still believed in the immortality of the soul.

18

Franz Schwartz was by then lying pressed against the wall of one of those sealed and boarded-up houses. In his mind, hovering somewhere between here and there, sounds and voices were converging and colliding, and only much later would he try to understand them.

In the Ascher house, which József Sárdy, secretary of the Office of the Special Military Tribunal, had just now, with an unfamiliar lump in his throat, been contemplating from the Hotel Dobray balcony, muffled laughter could be heard. It was like kittens at play tumbling out of a warm basket. At that sound, a forgotten softness climbed into Franz's arms, with the purr and even sharp claws of their Siamese, who at home he had had to shoo out of bed every night. He was clenching his frozen, disfigured hands as if trying to cling to this imagined, lost warmth. Even now he would be able to recognize that cat by touch alone, he thought, even blindfolded, but at the same moment he was overcome with anxiety: not for the life of him could he remember the cat's name. He felt an emptiness he had not been aware of before but which, over the past year, had been hollowing out a deep and terrifying pit in his memory, a pit into which his life was sinking.

That stunted black sign, which yesterday, on the doorstep of the hotel, had been spat from a woman's heart, was now shining in the mournful sky like a star. The faint light from this invisible eye had travelled thousands of years across the bleak and indifferent universe, only to be silently extinguished in the human gaze.

The woman, wrapped in a bright-coloured shawl, was still holding the cracked porcelain cup in her black hand, which seemed to have aged overnight. She was crouching in the middle of Main Square, her head sunk in her hands as if for the first time in her life she was grieving. No one could say what had crushed this otherwise wiry body. She was, in fact, one of the women who had always gone from house to house, and especially from coffee house to coffee house, telling people's fortunes. Nor could anyone say if there were several such women, or if it was only her they saw, a woman with different faces and hands, depending on whose palm she was gazing into.

For this dark gypsy hand was sometimes tender, almost a girl's hand, and at other times sharp as old leather. But everyone agreed that her vibrant, deep eye, which was like peering into a horrible dark sky, was always the same, always one and the same, and it was impossible to mistake it, let alone forget it.

19

The snow that came down on the lost and sleepy *varaš* in the middle of nowhere, that morning in late March 1945, would be the last thing they remembered when everyone who had stayed awake through that long night began to speak again. It was as if the fading eye hovering above the town was weeping. A white curtain was slowly descending on this forgotten world as if the final act of a never recorded tragedy had concluded. The silence that people had so long carried inside themselves, too long perhaps for a single lifetime, was now disturbed by a music nobody could recognize. It came from a wobbly cart trundling down the middle of Lendava Road, leaving dirty tracks on the thin blanket of snow. Weary horses, almost on their last legs, were pulling the driverless cart, in which rode a bois-terous company of musicians and drunken merrymakers. Running behind this cacophonous procession were barefoot children carrying a long red flag with its tail dragging in the mud down the rutted road.

The young fiddler – no more than a boy by his face – was still in good shape; he was standing on the front bench of the cart, thrust-ing his bow enthusiastically across the strings and bowing to the townsfolk watching this spectacle in alarm from behind the blinds of their upper-storey windows. The accordionist, reclining against the side ladder, was drawing the bellows with his eyes shut, as a third musician with a big drum simultaneously guzzled down cold *palinka* and beat out the rhythm of some forgotten melody.

'*Muzyka, tovarishchi! Muzyka!*' somebody shouted; he was among the ones lying on the floor of the cart gazing blankly into the grey, empty sky. The vehicle was wobbling past the abandoned synagogue when the man struggled to his knees, supporting himself with an officer's sabre like a wounded captain. He was watching the children, who were trying to catch up with this sinking ship but kept getting twisted and tangled in the enormous flag. And now they were giving up. Their battered, frozen feet knew instinctively that here, in front of this no-man's building (as the synagogue appeared to be), where somebody had made a fire, they could rest for a bit. They dashed out of the road, spread the muddy, rumpled flag on the cold ground and sat down by the fire, which nobody was tending.

'*Davai, davai palinku!*' a second man then said in a rasping voice as he pointed a pistol at the glass that was still being emptied down the drummer's throat. At the sight of the gun, the drummer choked and the liquor went up his nose and into his windpipe. Now everyone was laughing, even the ones who up until now had been absently counting the falling snowflakes.

In gusts and swirls – it was like watching a river drunk on melted snow from some invisible mountains – the wind was attacking the town on every side. The imaginary levees, behind which the virtuous, silent townsfolk had been sleeping these past years, had begun to give way. Few if any heard this wailing and whistling, borne by some unknown force. This concerto for pipe organ, more terrible and mighty than the music that had once resounded in the universal church, was now sowing genuine fear in their bones – not of righteous judgement or perdition, but of the hell that exists only here, solely inside us.

But still: something else could be heard as well, if only by one or two – for it was not the voice of the lonely, the lost and the hopeless; it was something that had the power to call forth sadness but not death, something capable of elation but not drunkenness. It was that forgotten but never lost melody of which only love is capable.

20

'Where did *they* come from?' snorted Benko, the factory owner, looking out at the street. He was standing behind a silk curtain in his large office, from where he had a fine view of Lendava Road, now white after the late-season snowfall. His head, sleepy and cold, still rang with the colourful billiard balls he had been shooting late into the evening at the Hotel Dobray. He suspected that there would soon be shooting in town. He was, after all, one of those rare well-informed gentlemen who had widespread connections, not only in Budapest but also in Belgrade, London, Berlin and Zadar. These past four years he had managed to hold on to something of what he had accomplished before the war began. The huge deals he had made as the director of an extremely successful meat-processing plant had taught him that when you play and sell big, you can't pick and choose your customers by their flags or beliefs. So he traded and made deals with anyone who, when it came to business, saw mainly money – not people and their trivial details or current political persuasions. Everybody eats sausages and ham, he would usually say to those who accused him of being too entre-preneurial and, as they put it, not caring who he did business with or where. For it was well known that he was the only supplier who had permits to export his meat products, which, by the way, were excellent, as even those who envied him or simply couldn't afford his merchandise had to admit. He had received licences from every-one – from the Germans as well as the English and the Hungarians, and of course from the Yugoslavs, too. From time to time, though not often and only when he had had a glass of that good Lendava white (for which he also had big plans), he would joke to Ruslanov, his loyal plant supervisor, that generals on all sides die with his sausages in their belly. And indeed, he had no lack of orders, or for that matter praise, from every front and battlefield, which he took as a particular honour. He had also made no little effort with the Americans, who, he calculated, would be delighted by his patented tinned ham, which was ideal for the long transoceanic crossing. He was sure that only now was his time truly arriving. Everyone here would probably be fighting each other a long time, whereas modern America would know how to appreciate his contribution to health and well-being.

He watched what was happening in the street with a peculiar, indefinable feeling in his stomach, which was in fact still empty. He had not even had his coffee yet, because for some inexplicable reason Ruslanov was late. It was also cold in the office and he was thinking that when he finally showed up he'd have to give him hell. The stove wasn't lit, and this damn snow still wasn't over and he was waiting for his coffee – it was all extremely unusual. His first thought was that Ruslanov must be somewhere in the yard buying pigs and horses for the slaughter and had been detained by the farmers, who were probably demanding exorbitant prices again, even though he had recently told them himself that now wasn't the time for such games since the days were coming when they'd have to grit their teeth and bear it if they wanted to get by. He'd made them a lot of promises, although he also knew that, with the war winding down, he would soon have to go back on the road if he wanted to secure new markets. He was already thinking of the future, when this vast region would see the arrival of new masters and their governments. But, as always, he was an optimist; he believed in nothing but common sense and commercial interest, as he liked to say.

It was Monday, the day they were purchasing large numbers of animals, since they were planning a new line of horsemeat products. Here, too, the most successful industrialist in the land was thinking of new business opportunities. He was banking on the worn-out and injured horses the armies would no longer need and would have to get rid of: they would provide him with cheap and, indeed, good-quality ingredients for his sausages. Thus he'd be able to fulfil the higher demand for meat when the men returned to town (he knew very well that after the years of hunger appetites would increase), because there would be a shortage of pigs for some time to come – the farmers were unwilling to adopt the kind of mass feeding system he had heard about from his foreign colleagues. He dreamed of establishing amid the cornfields, here in this flat and backward land, a large-scale pig-farming operation.

He and his plant supervisor, Ruslanov (who still wasn't upstairs), had driven through a large part of the surrounding land on their Sunday outings in his car, a vehicle of which he was extremely proud. Sometimes he would take his family with them, his wife and son, who, however, were not particularly enthusiastic about his bold if eccentric business plans: for them, all this driving past endless fields, and then walking along the remotest dead pools of the Mura, was little less than torture. Even their lunches, in some country inn or pub on the outskirts of town where they were usually served their own Benko sausages with seasoned potatoes, or maybe Hungarian paprikash (made with Benko pork), by now held little attraction for them. Benko himself – esteemed gentleman, factory owner and known to everybody as 'the boss' – always had a fresh cut of meat or handsomely labelled tin sitting in the boot of his new car, with which he would bribe the proprietors, extorting their fawning attention, and sometimes a free meal, too, while promising them a discount on, as he liked to say, 'exclusive' meat deliveries, even to the person's home. People who didn't hold such modern, enterprising views saw in his methods only greed and an underhand path to wealth.

'Well, my dears, you see what our land is like. The Mura is full of fish, and good for bathing, too, but no one takes any advantage of it,' Benko would say to his family over lunch in the garden of one of the many country inns from which they could see treetops in the distance, swaying in the summer wind or bending towards the river beneath the weight of numerous birds.

'All right, but then why don't you ever stop anywhere, so you and mother could have a bathe and I could cast a line in the river,' his son would argue, 'instead of driving us around in this muggy heat, when even the land just wants to have a rest.'

The son, called Jožek – though he was already an adult and well into his twenties – was being groomed to take over all these great enterprises one day, but he did not appear to like the idea. What he did appear to like was white wine and fashionable liqueurs, and of course 'the girlies' (as he called them). Benko knew, for he had been informed by a number of gentlemen, eagerly and with gleeful spite, and by some of his employees, too, which especially pained him, that his son was seen frequently, maybe even regularly, at the Dobray, where after an hour of billiards in the casino he liked to have a cuddle with Laci's little ladies.

'Be quiet, dear boy. You mustn't speak that way in front of your mother,' Benko interrupted his son. 'Besides, it wouldn't be right for us to bathe here; that's for people who have nowhere else to go. Your mother and I holiday on Lake Balaton, at our own place. Rozika, tell our son what it's like there.' He was trying to get on his wife's good side.

'Yes, it's lovely. But I do feel sorry for the boy, the way you're pushing him into the business.'

'Please, let's not get into that now. It's Sunday, and we've seen so many nice things,' Benko said, adding in the same breath: 'Our horses could graze out in the open here.'

Benko – factory owner, meat wholesaler and former mayor of Sóbota – was gazing across the dusty, desolate plain as if he was admiring the most beautiful mirage. He could feel the heat vapours, which were baking the earth and later, as evening approached, would sink into the slow, silent Mura. Having grown up here, he was familiar with these mirages, these apparitions of souls, but what now flared inside him was something much more material, something that dampened the fire in his eyes. Nobody could see this better than his wife, who was silently trying to follow his thoughts but was only getting more and more lost. She sensed that her husband no longer possessed his youthful softness and those enticing shadows, and that now inside him were merely ever more audacious schemes and business opportunities, accompanied by shady politics. It was the only life the man had.

'This could be big business for all us Prekmurians,' he said in a visionary tone, and with the unmistakeable enthusiasm that had once made him so attractive.

This was the last time, perhaps, that his wife, for whom he had long been lost, would see in his eyes the glow of his heart, which is what local people say when they mean you have a soul; or maybe she just so badly wanted to see it.

'So, Ruslanov, you're the only one who understands me – it's not easy for us either, is it? Pour us a glass of that cold Lendava wine, if our host says it's so good.'

21

And so, József Sárdy, secretary of the Office of the Special Military Tribunal, was thinking about death. He still stood, almost humbly, next to the well-worn billiard table, on which a naked female body was softly breathing. Above them, a gas lamp was droning as it bathed the table in a dim light.

The casino on the first floor of the Hotel Dobray was basically a ruin. Only a month or two earlier, although no one remembered it now, the upper crust of Sóbota (those who could still afford it) would come here regularly in the evenings; they were often joined by workers and farmers who had made some money in town and had come here to pour it down their throats. But people's greatest curiosity, which later gave rise to rumour and malicious gossip, was reserved for the strangers, the various newcomers and travelling salesmen, as they normally called themselves, although no one ever learned what had really brought them to this forgotten *varaš*, now when the world was going mad and in flames. They would usually have music played at their table, and sometimes paid big money for it, so that the musicians would later be talking for weeks, in whatever rural roadhouse their path took them to, about the fine gentlemen they had played for in town. All these stories, of course, excited to no end the imaginations of those simple, impoverished people, who had never dared to dream out loud.

It would also happen that one or another of these fine gentlemen in white turtlenecks and black overcoats, who ordered rounds of drinks for their table, even for people they didn't know, or gambled extravagantly at cards, or at billiards with the town elite at their regular table (which, they would say in their modern way, was a special precedent), were not to be found when Laci searched for them in the morning to settle the bill.

Most often, however, it was the ladies who were left disappointed and in tears by these freethinkers, petty thieves, smugglers or even deserters, who passed themselves off as travelling salesmen. In the middle of the night or towards morning, when fatigue and alcohol had gradually taken their toll on everyone, these mysterious gentlemen would whisper in a girlie's ear, and in her soul, that they had just one more big sale waiting for them in Vienna, Budapest or Bratislava, and then they would stop here on their way back, by which time their sweetheart would have to decide: was she going with them or staying?

By morning, of course, they had vanished with the first breeze.

József Sárdy, secretary of the Office of the Special Military Tribunal, walked over to the wall where the cues were hanging. Most of them were broken or warped, and some had no tips. Usually, at the sight of such indigence, he would have cursed the soldiers, the women, the drunks, who had no appreciation for such things, but now he was completely calm, almost pensive, as if preparing for a critical game, the last one that mattered. Everything else was forgotten.

He forgot about his half-debauched soldiers, who were crouching downstairs by the open windows and staring out at the dark, empty square. He forgot, too, about that butcher (as he called him) Mr Benko, with whom he had played billiards earlier that night. He no longer thought about his painful defeat or the deal Benko had offered him, which seemed dirty even to him. Nor was he even thinking about the body which lay exposed on the green baize, although now it was about her, too.

He chose the lightest, longest cue. There was a new chalk in the pocket of his uniform – the local elite would bribe him with billiard chalks for the right to play here. Everyone knew his vanity, and his spite, too, which could erupt unpredictably, and then he was even ready to shoot people, to kill them for no reason at all. Still, his moods had their weak points; there was something childish, almost infantile, lurking within the secretary (as they called him here behind his back). And people would feed this child billiard chalks, cigarettes, cognac and, especially, fine white stockings, which he wore beneath his boots.

Naturally enough, the problems with his feet could not be kept secret even from a town he had so long held in the grip of fear. Nothing could ever be kept secret in this town.

Indeed, not long after he arrived, women were already spreading the news that he had strange, smelly scales blossoming between his toes. Not even old slivovitz was much help for his condition, nor were the expensive curative lotions that shopkeepers and apothecaries supplied him with under the counter. So for a long time, from embarrassment, he would always sleep in his high officer's boots, even with women. The situation was more or less resolved by Sugar Neni, who was able only out of pure compassion to bear the sight and wretched smell of his afflicted feet. Every night without fail she would bathe his feet in warm water and apply a sweet-smelling lotion she herself had concocted, God only knew out of what. Mainly, however, she washed his socks. But it often happened that they were still not dry when József was required to go out in the middle of the night. Even though she knew he was leaving to look death in the eye, as he liked to say, and knew exactly what that meant, on such occasions she would roll her own fine white stockings up his legs. And he felt surprisingly good in them. After a while he didn't know what was helping him more: her bathing his feet or him wearing her stockings. Neni persuaded the finest shopkeeper in town, who despite the war was still able to purchase an ample supply of silk stockings, to get them for him on a regular basis.

The shopkeeper, of course, knew that the size she was requesting was not for a woman's foot.

József Sárdy, secretary of the Office of the Special Military Tribunal, was now wearing nothing but fine white stockings. From the pockets in the table he had selected three billiard balls – black, red and white. He had also removed the dressing gown and used it to polish the balls to a shine, as if he wished to wipe away all trace of other people's fingers.

Gently, he smoothed the woman's long hair around her pale face and placed the black and red balls on either side of her sleeping head. Then he picked up his light officer's pistol and, again using the dressing gown, polished that, too. He walked slowly to the bottom end of the billiard table and placed the cue ball on the mark for the break shot, just behind the woman's feet. He cocked the pistol and laid it on a corner. Then, for a long time, he rubbed the chalk on the tip of the cue and kept glancing at the table.

The woman still lay there without moving, her pinkish body now pinned between three billiard balls, which glistened in the light of the gas lamp.

22

The factory owner and meat wholesaler Josip Benko, hidden behind the silk curtain, was still gazing out at the street. In his hand he kept turning a valuable cigarette case, an heirloom he had inherited from his father, just as he had the business. He wanted to light a cigarette, but there was still no coffee. Now he, too, was no longer thinking about last night's billiard game, which in fact he had won, which normally would have pleased him, but still …

Mostly he was alarmed by what was happening in the street – although he realized something had to happen here soon and was prepared for it. For several days acquaintances, and his employees in the field, too, had been telling him that the front – which meant the Russians – was, more or less, just outside of town. But still he was surprised at how quickly the mighty German army had gone to the dogs. Only last night he tried to speak about this with the secretary, as he called him, somewhat bureaucratically to be sure, but Benko was an office type, a man of business, and military jargon was alien to him.

'We aren't going anywhere,' Secretary Sárdy had told him. 'We were sent to hold the town, and I can't just walk away from that. But if I do go, I still have plenty of birdies locked up here, and they're still chirping, so everyone will know when we fly away. But it won't be today.'

They were drinking the cognac Benko had brought him, one of his last bottles, and the game was moving fast. It was looking good for the secretary.

'I understand you, but my modest sources tell me that the front could quickly collapse now that Pest has been bleeding for such a long time. All I'm saying is we could come to an excellent arrangement where everybody gets something out of this. You have to think of yourself, too, especially now that you're not alone any more. Just in case, I mean.'

'Enough!'

Sárdy lost for the first time that night. His concentration had faltered, but Benko saw right away it was more than that. He had said something people didn't talk about.

'Well, let's put our worries aside, shall we? The night is still young.'

Across the street, on the other side of the muddy, snow-covered Lendava Road, in front of the abandoned synagogue, ashy grey smoke was rising into the sky.

Snow mixed with rain was dampening the fire, over which many frozen childish arms were extended. Benko deftly opened the case and pressed a short cigarette between his fingers. Not for a moment did he take his eyes off that fire. Despite the cold weather, the muddy barefoot children, only in shirtsleeves, were laughing and stumbling over the flag, which was getting more and more lost in the mud. The industrialist and meat wholesaler could feel that forgotten chill in some region of his heart. This was not empathy or pity – no one had ever taught him those things – but something much simpler and more immediate: for a brief second, in that spontaneous, playful mesh of children's arms over a dwindling fire he sensed human closeness, a warmth he had not known for a long time, and perhaps had never truly known.

The ship of fools had stopped beneath his window.

The fine rain, which as the morning progressed had been turning to snow, softened all words and muffled the distant explosions. In people's houses, too, everything for a moment became quiet; it was as though everybody in town who that morning was seen by the eye had, for an instant, looked up at it. But the only one who truly saw it, just as she had seen it in her hands, on the edges of the porcelain cup or simply in people's eyes, was her, the woman who, ever since yesterday and all through the long night had been walking around the forgotten *varaš* without really encountering anyone, for she had no one to whom she could tell what she saw.

Now she made one last circle and sat down in the middle of Main Square. She, too, was staring into the distance, still holding the coffee cup tight in her hand as if it was all she had left to remind her of home, a home she had never actually had. Her bed was this *varaš* and the countless paths she had walked far and wide, which each year anew were covered by earth or snow.

But that morning in March 1945 everybody felt, somewhere deep inside themselves, although they would never remember it later, that even the sky was weeping with them.

23

But the dwindling eye, which somewhere far away was growing darker above the *varaš*, as if it was dying, was not weeping. It was only snow, a late snow mixed with rain, watering the earth. A lullaby, whose message no one wished to understand, had long been rocking the souls here to sleep, like the voice of a mother who wants to protect her child from the truth. But now this beautiful voice was fading, and somewhere on the invisible edges of the plain that was eating into people's sleep, another voice was intruding – first as hope, then as distant explosions and finally only as fear, as if the dream had abruptly ended.

The town, this lost and forgotten world, in a world that had not been sleeping for years, was waking up, rising from its stupor, at the hour when death walks abroad, as people say.

Linna did not sleep that night, either. Her narrow bed, in a dark corner with a view of the inner courtyard, at the end of a corridor in the Hotel Dobray, was cold and covered in feathers, which all night had been falling out of sliced-up pillows.

'Tell me your name and I'll give you your pistol,' she said seductively, as only she knew how to do.

'Hand it over, I say! Don't play these games with me.'

'Just say it, darling, and you'll get your little toy.'

Linna was sitting on the edge of the bed, hiding the weapon behind her back. He was still in the doorway, looking at her. His face was turning red and he could barely gulp down the saliva that had suddenly gathered beneath his tongue.

'Hand it over or …' he barked as he dropped his cigarette and furiously ground it beneath his boot. He was still speaking when with all his strength he leapt at her.

Quickly, almost instinctively, the woman got to her feet and jumped nimbly away from the bed. The man tried to grab her but was too slow. He tumbled against the edge of the empty bed and fell to the floor as if slain.

'You can't even catch a girl, and you want to have a gun!'

The light stealing into the room through the wide-open door was like some translucent hazy thing. Everything that had been resting here so long, immersed in semi-darkness and silence, was slowly acquiring contours. A scent of abandonment hung in the air, as if the time that was trapped here had only now begun to stir. Every object smelled of rotting plants and dampness. Unfinished wine glasses still stood on the table, with flies lying in the thick, brownish residue inside them. Next to the window, a family photograph was scarred with mildew, which was growing beneath the grimy glass.

Yellowed papers, documents and ledgers were everywhere, as well as photographs and letters, as if someone in a hurry had been sorting through them, separating what was important from what was unimportant, the precious from the worthless, and, above all, memory from oblivion.

In the corner behind the door, where the light did not reach, stood a forgotten suitcase, a woman's handbag and a large, carefully wrapped package. These things had probably been prepared far in advance and safely stored here, and the person who had done this had probably sensed, even expected, that one night it would be necessary to leave; maybe he was making preparations for them to leave, to go somewhere far away, but it had all overtaken him; or maybe he had merely put off their departure, or wanted them to hope that they would never truly have to leave.

In other words, everything looked as if somebody had just left. The door was wide open, as if the traveller was planning to come back and retrieve his bag and the forgotten documents before he locked up for good. But he had only been able to take what he could lay his hands on. Or better, only what might separate a nameless person from the nameless.

It was as if the two people who were now staring wordlessly at each other had also been seen by that eye. For the first time, she noticed his puffy face and those eyes, tiny and shallow, which looked as if they had been living in the dark. His small, hunchbacked body was crawling on all fours. His strong, veiny hands were clawing at the filthy floor with short, chubby fingers, and his feet, in boots too high for him, which came up to his knees, were stomping furiously. He looked like an imaginary beast, a monster in a painting, the kind which, according to a local saying, everyone encounters at least once in their life.

He crawled beneath the table and just sat there. She stood on the other side of the room as if frozen, holding the pistol in her cold hands. She sensed that her time had come.

The light, that translucent hazy thing, evaporated before it had the chance to flood Ascher's house. Everything that for a moment had risen out of the darkness, as if wanting to shine once more, desperate to flee oblivion, was again fading before her eyes. Shadows had fallen on the unfinished wine glasses, voices were swallowed in an odour of staleness – which happened even before the faces in the dusty family photographs could open their eyes.

24

They had been lying motionless a long time, with a pillow over their heads as if they were trying to bury themselves, to sink into the earth or hide from that invisible eye (which in fact was not looking at them) or simply disappear from this world, when Linna suddenly pulled the sweaty pillow off their bodies and said, 'I'm gonna get us out of here, to somewhere …'

Kolosváry didn't hear what she said, or maybe he just didn't understand, although he was doing his best to catch something of it. Or maybe he was distracted by that unusual, determined tone, which he had never heard her use before, but in any case he continued to lie there motionless, on his back, as if encased in his own world. His eyes were shut and he was trying to keep the light far away. Whatever he was then seeing or imagining – because she wasn't sure if he was really asleep or simply daydreaming – she would never learn. And as if realizing this, she slowly lowered herself off the bed, again covered his face with the pillow and went over to the low attic window.

Evening was coming. Far beyond the last houses, somewhere along that line which, as her soldier liked to say, nobody had ever drawn, although some, he had heard, had reached it but hadn't yet returned to tell us about it, something was thickening, shining, glowing red. Reflected in her eyes, the line was opening, growing, speaking to whoever was listening.

The courtyard below already lay in semi-darkness; the shadows of the bare trees and scattered objects – crates and empty barrels, the broken hotel furniture the night watch outside used as kindling for their fire – had disappeared, or rather, come alive.

From here she could see almost nothing else, but all the same she felt something was moving, was hiding and watching from behind the corners. It was that forbidden time of day, the hour when everything seemed to settle down, when the streets emptied and beneath the few lamps that hung above the roads there really was nothing to be seen except fear, which itself was empty – although by now everybody knew that this emptiness, too, was just an illusion.

Because you really had to be blind or insane not to see the shadows, which, without leaving tracks, as if crawling over water, were moving, slipping, darting between the houses. More and more often they could be seen (at least that's what people said and we have to believe them) meeting – the shadows, that is – directly under the street lamps.

Linna waited patiently as she peered into the darkness that was veiling the town beneath her. Her soldier, beneath the pillow, was breathing peacefully, as if their hearts, which just a minute before had been pounding in their chests, calling to them, asking to be taken in their hands, had now grown calm, quenched their thirst and submerged into a long darkness. Then in the courtyard something moved.

He knew things would be easier if he was dead. Now there was no point uncovering his face, let alone asking questions. Either of himself or of her. Beneath the low ceiling, directly over his head, in the darkness in which her eyes alone were glowing, as if the line in the sky had got caught in them, that creature was moving.

It wasn't Linna any more and he was no longer her soldier Kolosváry. He had to get used to this, to adapt, but he couldn't do it, he felt. Now, when everything was slowly going to hell – this army, this war, this town and this depraved hotel, too, where nobody knew any more who was with whom, or who you were fighting against – he felt that he, too, could not hold out much longer. Him, her soldier, Kolosváry – all he wanted now was to somehow keep this love going.

When she kissed his pillow-covered forehead, it both chilled him and set him on fire. He felt her soft lips burning through the pillow, penetrating deep inside his skull, to where the word *love* was just coming into being, like a gleam in the middle of emptiness.

He knew about her frequent, mysterious absences from the hotel, which she was never able to, or never dared, talk about. 'You, too, my little soldier, are only human. Let me do this. The only thing that's worth my going out there is you. Know that I'm always going out there for you. All I ask is that you don't turn around, don't look to see where I'm going, because you won't find me there. I am yours, you know, I'm the way you want me, only when we're under our pillow. But I hope it won't be long before our pillow, the pillow we hide under, is the big Pannonian sky. And I dream that one day we'll be able to hide, and even show our faces forever, beneath this sky of ours.'

Maybe he really was dead, only he didn't know it yet because, if for no other reason, he still felt that heat on his forehead, as if it had burned into the bone. Her footsteps and that quick, almost soundless bustling about the room, as if a ghost was darting around his head, the ghost of a woman who just a few moments before had been a full person, frightened in her body and determined in her soul, but who now had vanished, like a shadow in the glow of a different lamp, a lamp he must never look at, since, as she said, he was only human – everything had gone quiet now.

He could bear it just a second more, then he yanked the pillow off his face as if determined to disobey the command. He knew he was crossing a boundary, that he would turn into a ghost, a shadow that didn't feel. But he wanted to look into that lamp, to see what was forbidden, and he instantly forgot that he was only human.

And yet, in this tiny attic room at the end of a corridor in the Hotel Dobray, on that evening in late March 1945, there was nothing but darkness all around. Somewhere far away, on the other side of consciousness, far beyond the town, the sound of muffled gunfire and the echo of explosions could be heard, which seemed to be coming from the depths of the earth, for in fact there was no echo here; nothing here resounded, everything merely struck, knocked and faded away like words in an empty, hollow mind.

He lowered himself off the bed and crawled on all fours to the low window. He peered into the emptiness; by now it was impossible to make out any object, anything at all, in the hotel courtyard. Of course, he couldn't be sure that he really wasn't seeing anything, since maybe that's what this other, forbidden, non-human light looked like, but he sensed, or at least imagined, that something was moving down there, soundlessly, wrapped in emptiness.

It started running – the shadow, that is – he was certain of it; it was running across the courtyard, towards a figure that was waiting at the extreme edge of what was visible. Then, for an instant, something gleamed inside him, shining through him like a bullet through the head: he saw her embrace the figure, put her arms around his neck, kiss him in the very same place on the forehead where she had earlier kissed *him*. Then they both vanished, as if they had jumped into a lake, but the circles were closing only within him.

The town disappeared completely in the gloom, along with its narrow streets and squat houses, with that inscrutable sadness, and with those souls in which people, despite everything, still believed.

25

Snow was falling slowly on this forgotten *varaš*. A spring snow, he may have thought at that moment, although he had never had a feeling for words, nor was there room for them inside him. Although he knew this, it had never troubled him; he had long been convinced that what a man like him needed was reality and a good measure of common sense. Why this was so he had never really asked himself, although he had often felt, as he did now, watching the snow silently, almost indifferently, whitening the town, that maybe there was something more to it. It was a sense he had, nothing but a feeling, and he wished he had a word for it, but he didn't. It was like this at times when he was alone in this big meat-processing plant, which was his entire life. He had never, never at all – and anyone could confirm this – found anything in this work that might go against his inclinations, let alone his convictions or, God forbid, religion – but even so … It wasn't that he was a weak sort of person, as he liked to say about others, some soft namby-pamby; no, he wasn't, because if he was, how could he have accomplished all this?

But now, being caught unexpectedly in this snow, which was coming down regardless, and there was already a finger's depth on the ledge, something took hold of him. It would be too much to say it was emptiness, although that is exactly what he was feeling. Something, that is, that could never be filled by his bookkeepers, business plans, sense of responsibility, over-the-top publicity or grand politics, not even by the gratitude of the local poor, which

made no sense even to him – although he did in fact make dona-
tions to the poor, yet he had no word inside him for their misery.
Not even the flattery of his subordinates, his production workers,
as he called those dull-minded butchers, who were always whining
about how their knives and cleavers weren't sharp enough – not
even that reached all the way down. Yes, dull knives was what they
complained about whenever he and Ruslanov made their rounds in
the abattoir. Never money, never the cold, never the blood clogging
the cesspit. Only knives, the dull knives.

He was used to the cold – not this Pannonian cold, blown across
the plain by Siberian winds, but the other, the abattoir cold, in the
cold room full of pale, refrigerated sides of meat. That, in fact, was
where he had got his start. In the cold room and the small abattoir.
When his father, a meat dealer, was still alive. That was when he
himself started working in the abattoir.

But now, strangely, he was seized by some childish, long-
forgotten curiosity, which made him open the window and stick
his hand into the snow on the ledge. He squeezed a clump of it and
brought it back into the office. Although the office, still unheated,
was itself cold, and his hands were, too, he could feel, as if for the
first time, how the snow was melting. The ice crystals were like a
miracle he had never experienced before. They were slowly changing into drops of water, which trickled through his fingers. At that
moment a word went through his consciousness, a thought, which
seemed to him neither strange nor alien: *it's warm* – and then – *like
life*. But the wholesaler and industrialist, the former mayor of Sóbota,
Josip Benko, had nobody to share this with.

Expectation distracted him. The shouting of the fools in the
street was already here. His hand was now merely wet, dirty with
snow and with that inhuman, drunken noise, which he couldn't
understand. He knew it was what the end sounded like – grunting,

squealing, kicking and finally just muscles twitching and those big eyes trying one last time to catch the light of this world.

Damn pigs – the words were stuck somewhere in his throat when the padded door swung open and the real world came rushing into the room.

'That's not how we do it here!' he hissed under his breath, as if his throat had gone dry. 'What are you playing at? Where have you been? That's not how people enter my office!'

'There are Russians down there, Director! It's the end, the end, just like I told you. The Reds are here, and now we'll see the devil riding your spotless pigs!'

'Ruslanov, pull yourself together! How dare you shout in my office. What Russians? That can't be right, you Russian idiot! You've been drinking that *palinka* and warm blood with the butchers, haven't you?'

'Go down and look for yourself, you'll see! Horses that should be under the knife – they'll take them all from us, even if they're totally worthless. They'll take anything, just like I told you. They're communists, those devils!'

'Shut the door, shut the door! Now get the hell out of here, you and your Russians! Go! And bring the horses in. I don't want to lose a single one – I paid good money for them! Do you hear me? Go!'

'But don't you understand? They've got corpses with them! A whole cartful of corpses! And now they're tossing them into our entranceway.'

Josip Benko quietly shut the door and turned the brass key. For the moment he was alone again, and the silence was soothing. He wanted that peace he found nowhere but in his office, where he received only his most important clients; not even his wife and son were welcome here.

Jožek, his only child, with whom he had never got along as father and son, he received in the office only when the boy did some sort of damage to the business or, as Benko put it, brought shame on them. The stories of Jožek's numerous quarrels in coffee houses, or in pubs on the edge of town, when after a few drinks he'd get mixed up with card sharks and unsuitable women – he had had to hear all these stories from people who were nothing to him. 'You'll be the ruin of us! Everything will go down the drain – or down your throat. You're worthless! That's what I told your mother, but she always protects you, for God's sake. If not for her, you'd be out on the streets, or maybe I should have left you in Banja Luka, doing hard time in jail with those whores of yours; it might've taught you something about life!'

On that occasion, Jožek said nothing and, as if he could give no other reply, had merely gazed at the smallest photograph on the wall. It was hanging in a corner by the window. When the curtains were open, the picture was usually hidden by the thick silk fabric, and now he alone could see it. It was one of the few photos with all three of them; he must have been about ten at the time. He had often tried to remember the occasion on which the photo was taken, but he couldn't for the life of him, and he had neither the desire nor the courage to ask. It must have been something special or they wouldn't have had themselves photographed – his father always called the photographer for events he considered significant, such as the opening of a new division, the purchase of a new car, hunting parties, political rallies or meetings with important clients.

Normally it was just him in the picture. In this photograph, however, they were all present: father, in a hat and wearing a tie, was sitting in a chair in the middle of a vast field; little Jožek – himself – he was holding in his lap; mama, meanwhile, was standing next to them in a beautiful white dress with her left hand resting on his father's shoulder and a purse hanging from her arm.

The picture in the field was truly extraordinary. This distinguished family, dressed for a drawing room, a coffee house or church, had had themselves photographed in the middle of farmland. Clearly, it must have taken a while to choose the right spot; then they would have had to bring a chair with them and, of course, get the photographer and all his equipment there, so it was certainly a significant moment.

But in all of this, what bothered Jožek the most, and also excited him, was why his father had taken that big child into his lap; only now did he feel how contrived it must have all been, as if his father was trying to bind the boy to himself forever.

He gazed at his father and mother, unable to understand; then his eyes drifted to the edge of the photograph, where in the distance a double row of poplar trees was rising out of the plain. Now, when he was an adult and the awkwardness was still with him, he thought: They will still be growing long after we are gone.

26

That invisible eye sign, perhaps only fiction, mirage or consolation to those who still believed in its presence, was now fading. Somewhere high above this forgotten *varaš*, which for so long had been tangling itself into a ball of fear, deceit and furtiveness, silence could be felt, pressing down with its never fully comprehended weight and demanding an answer.

The wind was whirling and scattering tiny, icy droplets, which were falling out of the great emptiness. If at that moment anyone was open or responsive to such things, they must certainly have sensed something more in this, for within that whiteness, blown out of the very fog and obscuring all views and muffling every voice, prayer and sigh, death was speaking.

Although it was still early – too early for migratory birds and too late for crows, which now were seen only in the surrounding fields, especially in the morning, as they rose with the fog into the cold day – something was definitely in the air, something powerful and nameless.

Only much later did one hear – or possibly never, for ordinary ears – the angels moving over the land.

What they saw, we will never know.

Downstairs, in the dark vestibule of the Hotel Dobray, by the back door to the courtyard, Linna stopped for a moment. This is where she usually received her instructions about where to go. She was used to these secret journeys at night, which no one in the hotel must ever find out about, least of all her soldier, who was then still lying beneath a pillow in her tiny attic room, but something told her that things were different now. For the first time they had talked – and not as two people who go to bed together to forget, to lose themselves, just for the hell of it, simply because lust is strangling them, eating at them like death. Now, there was something different between them. Maybe it was just a sense she had, the illusion of something more than a simple ache, but she felt that there had developed between them a closeness that was strong enough to banish fear.

This man, who for the past year had been coming regularly to her bed, just like all the other soldiers, like this filthy, corrupt town and the whole perverted world that had spawned this misery and war – as she sometimes dared to think as she lay powerless on her back, staring vacantly at the ceiling covered in tiny, bloody insect stains – this man, Private Kolosváry, she was now able to look in the eye. There was something in his eyes she felt she needed, and the few, soft words he spoke rang with something that went straight from her ears to her heart, which was the only way she knew how to explain it.

Of course, for her, in a way, everything was already lost. She knew this, and she had heard it, too, and of course understood – even if these soldiers saw her as nothing more than a mute, hollow, blind, moist body, which as soon as it spoke or complained could be tossed into the street to be fodder for the tongues of Sóbota. But all the same, this woman understood everything very well indeed. She knew that the world was falling apart. It was only a question of days before it collapsed, this world based on lies, pain, adultery and suffering, and what was coming next was something people feared like the devil fears the cross.

Only no one was talking about angels.

But they were coming – the angels, that is; they would fly across the land. You only had to be patient.

If anyone was sure of this, it was Linna.

She would have cried out, started screaming, if she hadn't lost her voice. But the hand on her shoulder was squeezing, not strangling her. She collected herself and turned to face the person in the darkness. From the sound of the breathing, she sensed that there were two of them, and that, too, was unusual.

'It's time to go, the postman is waiting.' Laci the hotelier was trying to calm her, give her courage.

'Go where?' she said uncertainly, whispering as if she didn't want to be heard at all.

Then, turning, she took another step and peered at the shape standing in the darkest corner of the vestibule. She heard it searching its pockets, feeling for matches.

'It's all right, don't be afraid. Mr Benko is one of us,' Laci said, when, after a sudden scraping noise, a yellow flame illuminated the stranger's face. The woman recognized him at once – he was one of those who all these years, despite everything, had been coming regularly to the hotel, to play cards and visit 'the girlies', as he liked to say.

'Go where?' she repeated, louder now, much louder, as if in a hurry, as if she wanted to get out of there as fast as possible.

For she had smelled something she couldn't see: the aroma of fine, expensive tobacco, the kind smoked only by a select few with connections on all sides. You had to be connected with both the devil and God to get this tobacco, which exuded a fragrance and gave off a smoke that was mild, blue and intoxicating, like burning in hell and smoking in heaven. It swept over her, rising from her stomach, this nausea, a dull pain, but also laughter, wild laughter she could barely restrain. For she could see him, this gentleman, naked on his knees, his hungry, helpless eyes watching her, begging her to do it with him one more time, to fill his pipe one more time before he left.

'Take this, you'll need it,' the gentleman said and pressed a roll of banknotes in her hand. Everything went quiet, inside her and all around. If anyone knew what money meant, she did.

But as if things were different now, she took the money and thrust it into her pocket.

Thanks – the word was left unsaid somewhere.

'Now go. You're expected at Črnske Meje. Bring the man back to Sóbota and wait in the house with him until it gets light. And then may God help us.'

'Linna, be careful. This one's different, they say.'

'Goodbye,' she said and vanished into the dark.

27

The entranceway that connected Lendava Road with Benko's factory yard was full before seven o'clock that morning. Farmers who had driven their horses and cattle from remote villages to Sóbota were crowding into the narrow passage to escape the cold and the snow. The animals, thirsty and hungry and overheated from the long trip, were neighing and huffing with hot breaths, which rose as a stifling mist to the ceiling and mingled with the smoke of cheap tobacco and the smell of alcohol. All the farmers were tired; some of them had been up since three and a few hadn't slept at all. If you wanted to clean, brush and feed the animals one last time so they looked healthy and strong enough to take a year or two off their age at the butchery, you had to start the day early. But they weren't the only ones in this dark, narrow and smelly entranceway, which led to the abattoir yard; there were also children there. For them, this was a rare opportunity to go to the *varaš*, that distant town on the plain; it was, to be sure, a long journey on foot, but later their fathers would buy them fresh bakery rolls, honey biscuits or boiled sweets, and those heavenly flavours in their mouths would more than make up for the soreness of their bare feet.

But for now, these children were standing squeezed beneath the large heads of the horses, fidgeting with the leads, as if heaven that morning was dying in their mouths, while their fathers were covertly assessing their neighbours' livestock and negotiating with the butchers.

Those sleepy, tiny eyes, which kept looking distractedly at the animals as if they were all saying a silent goodbye – that morning nobody noticed them.

For livestock and people alike, this was always a significant day. Their livelihood in the coming months would depend on the kind of price the farmers managed to get for these pitiful and thoroughly worn-out animals. Now, as a rumour was rapidly spreading that the bloodshed was soon to end and new times were coming, nobody believed any more that this meant better times. And then there was Benko's new interest in horses – people were saying he would soon be offering less for them than cattle. Indeed, they had heard that when the Russians came they would bring new machines, which from then on would plough and harrow the soil, and the animals would die out anyway, so everyone wanted to rid themselves of these big and useless (if docile and beautiful) beasts. They also knew that whoever got here early and found that crazy Russian Ruslanov – the boss here – still sober would get a better price per pound of live weight than the fucker would later be prepared to offer, after he'd been imbibing blood and spirits with his butchers. That's when he really did look at the horses' teeth.

'Tomorrow we'll be drinking nothing but horse blood,' Ruslanov, the supervisor at Benko's factory, was saying as he mingled the warm blood and spirits beneath his tongue. He'd started bright and early that morning downing a few with the butchers. 'But I tell you, it won't be long before we're mixing it with your Prekmurian blood, and Hungarian blood, too, and even with our own, Russian, blood, which is sweetest of all. You'll see. You won't be able to get enough of it!' he howled at the foremen, who were picking up the cowpats in the yard, and wiped his mouth on the sleeve of his leather jacket.

He knew as if he sensed it, or had maybe heard it in a nightmare, that the end was coming. The time was near – it was only a question of when, on what morning, those voices he knew so well would come thundering into this sleepy town. He was afraid of that day, more than he dared admit – for he knew them; he, too, had been part of that mad chorus. He felt that same soul inside him, which neither blood nor spirits could calm. It was as if nothing had settled down in all the years he had been here; it had only gone quiet, hidden itself like a tempest. And now it was coming for him.

He smelled what had no scent, heard what was only murmuring, knew it – this Russian émigré, Ruslanov – because he had seen it.

He had fled here from the Reds, as he liked to boast, although nobody really understood what that meant, for the role he played here had never been one of victim or righteous man.

As soon as he arrived in these parts, he had made it clear that, while he was made of the same clay as most of the people here, he'd been moulded by different hands: he was the kind of person who knew no other dance than with the soldier's baton.

Supervisor Ruslanov, a man without a country, now pushed through the throng in the entranceway; they all pressed against their animals as, with his baton, he tried to clear a path for himself to Lendava Road. He could feel that there was something wrong this morning; usually, the first ones here were the smugglers, black marketeers and petty horse thieves – gypsies, as he called the whole lot of them.

'Damn gypsies,' he would snarl as he pushed his way to the exit. But it wasn't working this time. His path seemed to be blocked, clogged with horse stench and frigid bodies. It was as if he was drifting and couldn't breathe; the blood he had imbibed was pounding in his head, he was sinking into the earth, which clung to his muddy feet, and a glob of sticky saliva was accumulating in his mouth, forcing itself up his nose, which was full of human misery – but somewhere in the distance, high above the horses' blinkers, light was filtering into the entranceway: pure, silent and white as snow.

That, in fact, was his colour: white – such as he had never seen before, the kind you only see once.

28

All that Linna could see were the outlines of squat houses leaning into the darkness beyond the dry road ditches. They were riding slowly, so the murmur of the sand and the crackle of the gravel as it struck the spokes of the large postal bicycle would not call forth any curious eyes or alert the night sentries, who were sure to be lurking half-asleep in the bushes or dozing in the darkest of the ditches. She knew that the trip became more dangerous each time: for a while now there had been hushed whispers in the gardens, behind the walls and as night approached, when there really were demons moving from house to house – people called them spite, deceit, fear, silence or simply the devil – something was brewing here. She could almost smell the stench slowly rising, and with it suppressed passions, and with those, a lust for revenge, which was nothing but envy, the desire, now that it was clear as day that everything would soon end, to be there when it happened. She knew as surely as if she'd been warned that anyone who, in all these years of silence, had somehow found the courage to breathe, would now be devoured. She felt it more strongly and deeply than this sanctimonious *varaš* could ever grasp – here silence and patience were valued more than risk-taking, more than freedom itself, for which she was ready to make love even with death. And she had done it, too, although nobody here would ever understand.

Maybe it was then, as a cramp seized her entire torso, that she did not merely feel but knew for a fact that she had sold her body a long time ago, to whom, not even God knew any more, and that all she had left was her soul, which at that moment, as she shook from the cold night and the macadamized Sóbota road, was the only thing that was truly clean.

They were both of them silent, as if all accounts had long ago been settled. They were approaching the last houses on the edge of town and in front of them there was only the great darkness above the plain. Her body, hanging inert and numb from the crossbar of the bicycle, was seized by another cramp. She clenched her hands more tightly around the handlebars and stared out at the thunderless flashes of lightning, which parted the blackness into which they were sinking with every rotation of the wheels. She could feel his arm – he had quickly let go of the handlebar – circling her waist. Right then she was seized by another cramp, stronger than ever. She gazed into the sky as if it really was consuming her and held her breath, trying to squeeze inside herself. She shut her eyes and focused on the sound of a barking dog, which remained somewhere behind her, tethered on a short chain among the last of the houses.

Now they were outside the town; at any moment, the pedalling should cease and she would go on by herself across the fields. 'So tell me what it's like in there, in that filthy hotel?' the man asked, still pumping the pedals, although they had already passed the point where he usually stopped. She said, as if the words came from her stomach, 'You're not supposed to know. Maybe later. But let me get off now. Your men will start shooting if they see I'm not alone.' The man tightened his arm, clasping her to his body. He was wheezing from exertion and arousal, his thick hot breath tugging at his tongue, so he could barely get the words out: 'Who are you? What are you doing here?'

Linna had lost count of these nocturnal trips, travelling to the edge of town to fetch someone. She didn't even ask who they were or where they were going – she had realized a long time ago that was how it had to be. This was her way of searching for freedom, although she knew it was a word she could no longer share with anyone. But she had, in a way. 'Even I need someone to share the loneliness with; it's the only way to defeat it,' she had said, casually, as if she'd been thinking about it a long time. But she hadn't; it was as if her body was talking, as if pain had taught it how to speak.

The pedals stopped turning. Now the only noise was the rattling of the bicycle, which was slowing down but still rolling steadily towards the sky.

She heard an echo, as if the plain itself was answering her: 'Who are you' rumbled over her head in the thunder. The bicycle stopped; she felt the ground shake as lightning struck somewhere far away, or maybe this was an answer, a voice not for every ear.

She was back on earth.

In the darkest corner of the vestibule, by the back door of the Hotel Dobray, the two shapes still stood in silence. The door was cracked open, allowing a thin line of light to slip into the room and draw an almost invisible boundary.

'It's the same with us, my dear Laci,' Benko said in a decisive if somewhat hushed voice. 'Here, we divide ourselves up into groups; there, God divides us, every man according to his deeds. And nothing can be done about that, not even the pope can change it. That's all I wanted to show our people. But they didn't want to hear it when I told them you just have to work and things will be all right. For me it was never about politics, and it's not now, either. Politics comes and goes, but something else remains.'

'We're both businessmen, Mr Benko; we have to work for every-one,' Laci the hotelier said and roughly exhaled the tobacco smoke, which he wasn't used to. He had never been a smoker, but now even he had to unwind. The line of light in front of their feet, as if separating them from the mad world, had in the smoke become a diaphanous wall. Again they fell silent, as if each man was gazing at his own hallucination.

'By now she's with them, on the other side,' the hotelier said, almost whispering.

'What a beautiful girl that one is. Sometimes I think they should all look like that. But then I think it'd be best if none of them did.'

Benko quickly lit another; he was afraid of that illusory wall vanishing, which, at least for a moment, was protecting them from what was on the other side.

'True, but I'm more and more worried about my girls, about what will happen to them tomorrow, when they finally do have freedom.'

'What freedom? What are you talking about? I tell you, you have no idea what's coming to our *varaš*. Believe me, I've seen what they're planning.'

'Really? Can there be anything worse than the shambles I have upstairs? And this is supposed to be order and discipline! Nobody respects anyone any more, it doesn't matter if you're a gentleman or a country bumpkin. You can't even find a decent musician these days.'

'Wait a bit, Laci, you'll see. If our girl makes it through the night, we can treat ourselves another time, to music and to girlies, too.'

Again the two men fell silent. All that could be heard were smacking lips and puffing on tobacco. But the wall that was protecting them they could no longer keep building. That faint light had gone out and now an entirely different light pierced the vestibule, strong and blinding, ready to devour and destroy any illusion that might still be hiding or lurking somewhere.

The lightning flash, released above the open land, permeated every cranny, every seedy cellar dive and even dreams. The back door was blown shut with a bang and the vestibule was glowing.

The smoke burst into long tongues of bluish flame, which burned away the masks from the faces of the men, who stood there naked, like Everyman.

They knew they needed each other now.

We must keep together and trust each other, Benko thought when they were again in the dark and there was only rumbling outside. At that moment, they could not tell if it was thunder or if the shooting had finally started.

He wanted to talk more about the woman, and also about the letter he was carrying in an inside pocket. But now Mr Benko, factory owner and meat wholesaler, no longer trusted anybody.

He believed what he had been taught: you had to mind your own business, do your own work and God will help you. He had thought about God more than once that day, which in itself was something.

So he left.

'I'm going to check on József. I'll be upstairs with him. You go back to those debauched soldiers and fill their glasses one last time. Tomorrow everything will be different.'

29

That morning the Hotel Dobray, when the fog that surrounded it finally lifted – or maybe the fog was only in the eyes of those intoxicated, sleepy mariners, who had spent the whole night leaning at the windows with their rifles – resembled nothing so much as a ship run aground. It was slowly sinking into the mud, which was covered by the snow that had started coming down as morning approached.

That hotel, in the middle of town, might indeed have sunk into quicksand, leaving in its place a void encircled by tall chestnuts about to sprout new shoots – if nothing had shifted then.

For the earth, when it opens, claims its own.

And when it starts to open, it keeps opening for a long time.

And then it devours both good and evil without distinction.

This is what the hotelier Laci, the last person here still in his right mind, was thinking, pondering, weighing and calculating, but he, too, now found his thoughts getting away from him, as he decanted the last litre of *palinka*, trying all the time to keep a steady hand.

He was standing behind the counter, where truly nothing remained. The last of the glasses were in pieces from the night before, but in the pocket of his black waistcoat he had hidden a small carafe, as if he wanted to rescue some memory of the galley that was lying forever at the bottom of the sea. For he could sense that they were slowly taking on water. Water, like an invisible, inaudible force, was pouring into this filthy stable and relentlessly drowning the listless, insensible animals, who despite the danger were still crouching devotedly in their stalls, gazing at the mirage on the wall.

As if their chains, which existed solely inside them, had long ago been tightened.

It was day outside when Private Kolosváry laid his dull bayonet on the wooden floor beneath the window in the Hotel Dobray. He stood there in front of the open window, gazing at the carvings in the wallpaper. As if transfixed, he was admiring his horses, who were grazing in a boundless grassland no one but him had seen. The animals, forged from imagination and homesickness, from memory, were calling to him, as if for a moment a landscape had opened that did not exist, a boundlessness you enter only if you are mad or dead.

He didn't know any more which category he belonged to.

It was pulling him, irresistibly. It was a voice bursting in from Main Square, from outside this miserable, depraved hotel, and at the same time it was a voice speaking to him from within, sounding like his conscience, like something you must never lose. It was as if he had to decide, before leaving forever: go mad or die?

Private Kolosváry had carved his first horse in the wall of the Hotel Dobray after he returned from Linna's attic room. All night he had been tormented, gnawed at, by the thought that when this madness, this war, finally ended, he would be alone again. In his head he kept hearing: 'I'm gonna get us out of here, to somewhere,' but she had never come back last night. All night he was walking up and down the corridors, although it was forbidden and he risked running into József Sárdy, who now, when everything was going wrong, would certainly have shot him for this innocent transgression. But the soldier couldn't help himself. He still felt that kiss on his forehead; it burned more painfully than the blisters on his hands. He was carving, with ever greater determination, as if in the picture on the wall he saw a way out, somewhere he and his Linna could run away to. He would never learn that she, too, was trapped, very close by, in a house that was more or less across the street. So, in the end, all he had were these carved horses, pictures that no one but he, the Hungarian soldier, Private Kolosváry, could understand.

The horses were getting closer and closer; at first, they became agitated as he slowly approached them. He knew he was alone here, that there was nobody to stand by his side, nobody to protect him, to make excuses for him; for the first time in his life he would have to do that for himself. He was standing in the middle of the plain, which in the distance touched the sky; he seemed to be floating above a trench – he could sense this scar, this never-healed wound, out of which he had grown. Now it was time to return the thing he carried inside him – this silence.

The animals were surrounding him, gazing at him with their big white eyes as if they understood. He reached out his arm and offered them his hand. It stung and it burned, deep down, as the bloody blisters opened. The blood was trickling between his fingers, which all this night, all his life, had been digging carvings into the wall.

'Damn it, man, what are you doing? You idiot!' cried the soldier Géza. His head was pressed to the floor, ever since that first sharp pop when something came flying in through the open window. 'Get down! Didn't you hear it?' He was pleading with Kolosváry, who remained standing at the window holding out his bloody, blistered hands, neither asking nor granting forgiveness.

Then, again, that whistling, which was caught in the chandelier. Another sharp pop, and pearls, it seemed, were spilling into this pigsty.

Laci the hotelier listened to the popping, the smashing, the clattering, which he still did not understand. He was kneeling behind the counter, guarding the little carafe. At the first pop, which landed rather far away in the back wall and took a while to get there, he didn't believe that a bullet could ever bring this place down. It was as if a void had formed here; they were trapped in it and would never leave. He had felt time trickling slowly through the narrow neck of the funnel, as again and again he decanted, poured and emptied the liquor, here, with these soldiers, in this hotel, which God, justice and civilization had forgotten.

Then, even before it became quiet and the popping faded away, in this hollow space of no dimensions, as if open only to silence, to the depths of the plain that surrounded this hollow *varaš*, this mute world attuned only to sky and earth – then, for the first time, the telephone rang.

But nobody answered it.

And it kept on ringing. At first just in the hotel, but then throughout the entire town, as if this was now truly the end of the dream.

30

The magic of the brass key was working again.

Benko did not often lock the door – even when engaged in confidential conversations or making deals that were not entirely above board, he might leave the door open. This gave him a feeling of strength. Openness, he believed, was his most powerful weapon. In this factory – in this town – he was boss, and he knew how to show it. Open doors, open curtains – it all sent fear into the hearts of the various black marketeers, small-time smugglers and blackmailers who tried to do business with him under the table. He let them know that business was business and a man's word meant something here and couldn't be twisted or revoked. So people of every background spoke of him with respect, even to excess.

But this morning was different for Mr Benko. He wanted to be alone for a moment, with his thoughts and plans, of which he still had so many. Today was the first day of his large-scale purchase of horses, and tomorrow they were supposed to begin the production of horsemeat items. That was how he would resolve the issue of the raw materials needed for broadening production: he was counting on the fact that the demand for meat and meat products would rise sharply after the war, but there weren't enough pigs and cattle in the farmers' barns. Horses, for God's sake, horses! How was it no one had ever thought of that before? he had often flattered himself. And later, on the Mura, which now flowed by without any real benefit, he would set up a pig farm and start raising animals on a large scale, and since there would be water nearby and empty fields, they wouldn't be thirsty or hungry. Such thoughts were constantly spinning round in his head. Up to now he'd been convinced that neither politics nor any government could stop him from doing this. After all, as he always said, he wasn't doing these things just for himself but for the common good as well. There's real potential here, there's money in it – was how he put it.

And now the horses were here and Mr Benko, large-scale industrialist and unrivalled entrepreneur, had no idea what he was going to do with them.

He sat there in a daze in his gilded cage, thrice locked with a brass key. He could feel that the devil was near, although he knew this was nothing but a story.

Amazingly, the shouting, the neighing and, especially, that tuneless drunken music seemed to have calmed down. It had receded deep in the background, far from his thoughts, far from here. He was again fascinated by the snow, which was steadily coming down on Sóbota; he gazed at the town through the misted window as if he was somewhere else. He watched as this forgotten town, with its squat little houses and covered windows, its bell towers and muddy, crooked streets, was slowly turning white, being hidden by the snow. The town seemed to be lifting itself, rising on long stilts, which, beneath the houses, had sprouted out of the silence, the patience and the boredom. It kept rising, and was already as high as the bell towers of both churches, so that in the snow below nothing remained but black, flattened patches of land. The *varaš* was suspended somewhere between sky and earth, supported only on thin wooden legs. He felt the clouds, the fog, floating beneath the rescued town. Now it needed only to make a step, to move forward and cross to the other side.

But here, now, there was no one who would go. He clenched his hand, which a moment before had seemed warm, heated with childish enthusiasm, and thought: this nest will fall again.

He took a cigarette from the case, or maybe it was still that first one, he didn't know any more, and raised it slowly to his dry mouth. But now his hand was again cold, heavy and shaking. Just so – his.

Across the street, only thick, greyish smoke was rising from the damp embers. The muddy children were stomping their bare feet in the snow and stretching out their hands over the fire. He saw their taut throats and open mouths, which were shouting. But he could not understand or hear anything.

He placed his hand on the cool window latch and turned – once, twice, three times. Nothing. The window remained hermetically sealed. The latch was jammed, it wasn't working, which had never happened before.

If the world had been the way it was only yesterday, Mr Benko, large-scale industrialist and former mayor of Sóbota, would by now be yelling at his chief supervisor, Ruslanov, to fix it for God's sake, but everything was different now. Ruslanov was somewhere downstairs, trapped in the entranceway or drinking blood with the butchers. It may have been then, at that very moment, when a sharp pop rang out. With that, perhaps, single shot, which ripped the morning in two, Benko's world ended – but he did not know this yet.

Now, with a kind of resignation, almost calm, he simply let go of the cool latch and was peering at the apparition that had emerged from the white background.

The man in the long army overcoat, which had once belonged to an unknown hero or deserter or only to a corpse, was slowly making his way towards the fire in front of the abandoned Sóbota synagogue. His dark, erased, nameless face was covered by a rumpled hat.

He could feel that this figure, walking through the soundless, empty space, on this early morning in late March 1945, was closer to him than he imagined.

31

The hotel corridors were dark that night. The soldiers, who would normally have been drinking and playing cards on the stairs or sitting in front of their women's rooms on the first floor, were now leaning, maybe half-dozing, at the open windows. Their rifles, which perhaps they had never yet fired and now would never again clean, looked like broken oars. The grounded ship was sinking into despondency and despair, into the sickness unto death.

In the corners, deep inside the ravaged coffee house, a few candles gave off a dim light, which cast long, flickering shadows up the walls. It looked like everything that belonged here was slowly moving out, was fleeing into the abyss. In this inscrutable painting, which would vanish as soon as the wind blew out the last tiny candle, something was hidden. But nobody here would notice it.

Slowly, with restrained step, Benko walked down the narrow corridor, from the back door to the staircase that led to the casino on the first floor. Only a few minutes earlier, when he was leaving Laci the hotelier, he had been full of confidence and pure thoughts. But now, as he stepped on the first stair, he felt a weight descending on his shoulders, pulling him down, so that every subsequent step he took grew heavier.

He held on to the wooden panelling, running his fingers over the names and dates, which had been scratched there every night by drunk, bored and despairing soldiers. It was dark on the stairs, but as he reached the top, where from beneath one of the doors, and only one, a light was shining, he found *her* name carved into the wall: *Linna*.

This, he thought, could be a good omen.

And then he thought: he had never thought like this before.

It was other sorts of omens that spoke to him, if any did.

Upstairs lay a ragged red carpet full of cigarette burns, on which the Sóbota elite had once walked back and forth on their way either to the casino or to the ladies, whose rooms stood along the corridor to the left. He went up to a window overlooking Main Street, as though he wished to delay for a bit his meeting with József Sárdy, secretary of the Office of the Special Military Tribunal.

Sóbota is already sleeping – he said to himself – same as always.

He gazed out at the thin rain; it was falling like invisible cords down which something was entering the town that most people had shut their eyes to – Josip Benko, too, the strongest of them.

He quickly looked away, as if wanting to flee, and his eyes fell on Ascher's house.

'They ought to be there by now,' he murmured.

Not even he could tell if this was a question or a command. It appeared calm there, across the street. The man he had not yet recognized – he would not see him until the morning and then through a different window – was not visible from here.

Benko had been given a special assignment that night, the kind he had never had before, and so had Linna, but he did not suspect that this work, these nocturnal assignments, which neither of them would ever fully understand, connected them more than they could imagine – as they would soon find out.

For many years, going back long before the war, ever since he began his meat business, Benko had been a major player in the region – he always had striven to be first in everything, not just industry but society, too. He had founded and directed associations, hunting societies and sports clubs; edited his own newspaper; worked to establish a secondary school, to send students to university; was an active member of the Prekmurje Academic Club; and, not least, for a number of years he had served as the mayor of Sóbota and had been a member of the parliament in Belgrade, which meant that he travelled regularly throughout Yugoslavia – and was no less regularly seen in business offices, coffee houses and drawing rooms in the company of the finest women, in Budapest, Graz, Vienna and Bratislava. His business, which rapidly became one of the largest meat-processing plants not only in Prekmurje but far beyond as well, was only part – a strong and important part, to be sure – of the grand plans Benko had for this backward and, largely, still agrarian and petit bourgeois world, which he himself wanted to transcend.

'That's why you need to work hard, think for yourself and consider every dinar you spend,' he would say. Initially, he turned to his Lutheran brethren for support and confirmation of this idea – they had been helpful to him, after all, in his heated debates with the Catholics. That was why he had started his newspaper – to goad the clergy, especially through his defence of big capital and his rants against the excessive religiosity of the peasants and uneducated petit bourgeoisie, those people who had nothing except church, disease and poverty. But he soon saw that not even his brothers in Christ could follow him any more, so he found meaning solely in hard work, as if he believed that he, personally, could bring culture, civilization and self-confidence to this town, to this region forgotten by the world, trapped between the Mura and Raba rivers.

Naturally, in this struggle against ignorance and backwardness, which could not or would not understand that the world was changing, he sought allies in other quarters, too – on the other side, if it must be said, and on a third and fourth side – anywhere he found people willing to take a risk. Thus it became known that, very early on, even before he took over the business from his father (who was in every respect a notorious boss, a man who had sent generations of Prekmurians to labour at seasonal work in Vojvodina and Slavonia, on Austrian estates and even on French plantations), Benko had used his father's money to support not only the Jews but also that dubious Red of no provenance, that self-declared revolutionary, Vilmoš Tkalec – and he had been criticized for it ever since. It was here, in fact, from the balcony of the Hotel Dobray, on May 29, 1919, that Tkalec had proclaimed the Republic of Prekmurje, which existed a mere four days, until the Hungarians routed his army – more comical than serious, composed of peasants without land, proletarians without machinery, soldiers without officers and poets without inspiration.

And now, on this rainy night in late March 1945, nearly twenty-six years later, here he was, standing on this same spot, in front of this same window, on the first floor of the Hotel Dobray.

Sóbota was asleep – he again assured himself – same as always.

Soon it would be morning, and someone would again be proclaiming war or peace from the balcony of the Hotel Dobray, and he would again, as always, be standing in the background, with his reputation and his power and, especially, his money.

Even so – Benko suspected that this might well be his final battle, though he did not know it for sure yet.

32

She took off her shoes, which she had borrowed, and was stepping from the road into the field when the sky again flashed with lightning. For an instant, or maybe longer – to Linna it seemed an eternity – the town behind her, which a traveller might otherwise have missed, was completely lit up. And she, too, who was supposed to keep out of sight, to melt into the naked, open plain – she was now exposed, as if offering herself to the entire world. Even the earth and sky seemed to reproach her, to slander her, but still, inside, she was sturdier now, determined, clean – she didn't want to cover anything up or hide anything any more. Here, now, she was alone, and would go on like that to the end.

She felt the wind, that cold, sharp sweep, which had wormed its way among the houses and relentlessly burrowed into the souls of those who lied. She knew it was a force that could consume anyone. She knew those cold hands, how they grabbed and tore and wheezed. She would recognize them among millions of gentle, shy, even dirty and rough fingers, because there was nothing uglier than a body that was vacant, without feeling. She had seen and smelled these hollow, soulless creatures, how they just lay there, fleeing from something immaterial, invisible, something less than the wind, which always has its own voice.

Her assignment that night was to go to Črnske Meje, to the acacia woods, about halfway between the town and the Mura, the river where the 'illegals' (as they were called) either came from or fled to. She would wait for them in the woods, or more often simply fetch them from the ferrymen who carried them across the river. Then she would bring them to the town, along the darkest lanes, past gardens and over walls, normally to the Hotel Dobray, where they would spend the night, sometimes staying for days in rooms in the cellar.

Naturally, she never asked who these people were, who were travelling with suitcases and bags, on foot or on bicycle, mostly alone but sometimes with wives or girlfriends, or even with their families.

Sometimes she would let them use her own little room in the attic, and sometimes they would even sleep together. Usually, along the way, and later, too, she wouldn't say a word to them; everything took place more or less in silence, quickly, with no human connection. A few times women or children had spoken to her, although there seemed to be a basic agreement that the less they knew about each other, the better for everyone. But still …

Then, too, she did not speak foreign languages, although she had of necessity learned Hungarian and a few German words (from soldiers, of course) – but although these people spoke languages that sounded something like her own, they still couldn't understand each other. Nevertheless, in all of them, without exception, no matter whether they were alone or with others, old or young, well dressed or in threadbare suits or in uniforms, she felt the fear, homesickness or guilt – something that spoke to her even when it was buried in silence.

The stylish long overcoat with the fur collar and the last pair of high-heeled suede shoes that remained to the women at the Hotel Dobray she had borrowed from Sugar Neni. Now, with the shoes clutched beneath her left arm so they wouldn't get muddy or ruined, Linna took a few cautious steps over the cold ground. She wanted to get away as quickly as possible from the man, who had still not turned the bicycle around and started back to town. She felt his eyes following her in the darkness. She walked faster and faster, stumbling over large clods of earth and ploughed furrows, until she finally disappeared into the night and merged into the black field.

It was safer, she knew, to cross the open field than to walk along the road, where she might easily run into the night watch, or the deserters who hid in the ditches. It was said that there were more and more of these men, hungry, frightened and lost on the plain. They would travel at night, looking for a way out of this forgotten region that for so long had been in the middle of nowhere. But by now they all knew that this flat, endless land was under siege.

Fleeing east was no longer feasible: the last of the German and Hungarian border guards were already dying under fire from the Russians, who at dawn might well come storming across the plain. To the west, not far from where Linna now walked, the land was bounded by the Mura, which in March 1945 could not be crossed without a boat or raft. These, however, were still under surveillance by the occupying forces, who were on the lookout for deserters and would shoot to kill. They didn't dare go south, where it was already liberated. Handing yourself over to the Yugoslav Partisans was a risk only the most desperate would take. It was said that an order had been issued to shoot all prisoners and deserters, anyone in a different uniform, even their own men. So the only hope deserters had was to find their way north, to the Austrian border, where they could surrender to the British.

But which way is north, now, when they'd been hiding in ditches day after day, hungry, their nerves completely shot? When at night, beneath a starless sky, they'd been wandering in circles across the plain?

Linna knew exactly where she was and where she had to go, but even so, she felt a sense of foreboding now; maybe it was just an eye watching from the darkness. She hugged herself for a moment and crouched to the ground, as if it was possible to hide here, in the open, under nothing but sky. A raindrop trickled down her cheek, and another fell on her sweat-soaked hair. She looked up at the bright, flickering edges of the storm clouds: behind them, somewhere high above the earth, as if from the very stars, there were flashes of lightning. That's when she heard something rattling and jingling behind her. She ran like she was out of her mind.

33

The sky was completely covered. The plain was shrouded in thick darkness, as if in a shallow grave.

The earth, too, perhaps, had collapsed into itself that night, just as more and more often there were whispers that such-and-such a person had withdrawn into himself, had not spoken for a long time and only stared at you with pale, empty eyes. But people had been that way here from time immemorial – not unlike this silent, peaceful, inward-looking landscape, which in one way or another affected everyone who entered it.

All that could be heard were sounds layered in the wind, rising and dying in the sodden earth. Lightning was flashing, but only high above, in the black clouds. Somewhere along the perimeter of the land, which opened into a boundless expanse, only trees were rustling; it was like being trapped in a hollow, enchanted circle.

Driven by fear and footsteps she didn't recognize, Linna was now thinking only of some place to hide, to catch her breath or collapse. Črnske Meje, she sensed, could not be much further. But in the darkness and rain, which kept dissolving the furrows in which her feet were sinking, it was harder and harder to run.

And because she was running and at the same time ducking shadows, which kept rising in front of her as if growing out of the ground or from the ditches, or were simply there, she was always straying off course, going deeper into the field, which had neither centre nor perimeter. Then, for a moment, the sky opened again and the field was lit up.

She stood in a puddle and looked around. She couldn't make out the town any more; it had faded into the background. It seemed like she was closer to the road now, although this was more of a guess. In the distance, she saw only the big chestnut tree with the wayside shrine beneath it – if, of course, this was right road.

The air, which she could breathe again, and the cold rain on her lips calmed her. I could stay here, she thought; I'll wait a little, then take off.

But the old tree, the one she would usually hide beneath on her way from Sóbota to Črnske Meje as she waited for the road to clear, had vanished again in the darkness, as if it had been swallowed by some invisible force, or maybe it was never there and she was now looking at a different shrine, one she had never seen before; or worse, that wasn't real either and it was all just an illusion, an image forged out of fear, and this, too, would be washed away by the rain, and nothing would remain but what was real – so now there was no more tree, and in its place, somewhere deep inside her, growing, settling and taking root, only doubt.

And there was still that promise, of course, alive and real, like that shrine on the other side, which was the only visible thing in the night.

For she had said: 'I'm gonna get us out of here.'

And there was this, too: 'Be careful, this one's different.'

And last but not least: for the first time, she had money.

She had to make a decision. She could go on and do what she had been ordered to do, entrusted with and even paid for in advance (which had never happened before). Or she could set off now and find the path to the Mura, which she knew, and find a ferryman or one of the boatmen, who were sure to be hiding in the dead pools waiting for fugitives, smugglers or illegals – as the Partisans and political activists were called, who more and more frequently these days were crossing the river and organizing the too-long-anticipated underground resistance, even before the Red Army invaded the region. For everyone knew that the Russians were at the border. That very night, perhaps, they were preparing an offensive towards the Mura. If nothing else, you could hear the whistling of Stalin's mysterious pipe organ somewhere beyond the plain. So these nights the secret river traffic was, undoubtedly, very profitable. Everybody was in a hurry to cross. Some to this side, others to that side.

But as much as she was driven to go on, Linna was also pulled back. What the river was for some, the Hotel Dobray was for her. For within that wretched, filthy, insane hotel, in the middle of that forgotten *varaš*, her faith, hope and love still lay.

This she could neither forget nor abandon.

But before she could look around a second time, even before she could decide where to go and how, she was seized by a firm hand and knocked down in the mud.

She didn't see anything; there was only an echo inside her, resonating somewhere deep, like an earthquake. She was sinking into a crack, frantically clutching at the wet soil to keep herself from being buried, but it merely oozed silently through her fingers. She felt a tongue, sour and cold, digging between her teeth and getting caught in her stomach. She couldn't breathe; convulsing and hurting, she floated in and out of consciousness. Drifting, suffocating, pinned and strangled.

A knobbly hand was pressing behind her knees, ripping at her stockings; below her breasts, an enormous steel tube had dug its way inside her – it was like being nailed to the ground. Nowhere now was there any shrine or road, no world any more. And there was nothing moving above her, where she stared with white, vacant eyes, eyes that seemed to have gone somewhere else, so they wouldn't have to look at death, which must have been there all along, waiting, perhaps, beneath the old chestnut, hidden behind that wayside shrine, or maybe there really was nothing there any more.

One more thrust and her body would have exploded, would have suffocated in the mud, but the pressure let up for a moment, as if the point of the steel tube (a pistol, she thought) had got stuck somewhere, caught in her bones.

Again she heard that heavy breathing and those words, 'Who are you?', which seemed not to be coming from anywhere. The body above her was relaxing, wheezing; it rolled onto its side and began pulling her to itself. Her lips were free again; she was gasping for air, but her tongue, full of mud, was glued to the top of her mouth. The man again squeezed her around the waist, clasping her to himself, as if he wanted to break her in half. She opened her hand and tried to lift herself up on her now-free arms, which kept sinking into the soil. But before she fell back, somewhere deep down her fingers touched steel, the thing that only moments before had been nailing her to the ground.

Without making a sound, she pulled her hand out of the soil and, with a strength she had never felt before, swung.

She felt nothing bad; all that remained was a strange satisfaction and relief, like hitting a billiard ball.

34

The invisible sign, that chicken eye, which no one here noticed and maybe even the fortune teller had forgotten by now, was still somewhere above Sóbota. There, perhaps, it started clearing, cleansing itself, as if it had cried itself out, grieved over everything that was still to happen, for as people were saying: 'The worst is yet to come.'

Benko, who had been walking through the empty, silent, sodden streets, did in fact feel that now, somewhere, it must be getting clearer, but this was more in his head, in a world deep inside him, where nobody could have followed him that night.

If his body had not started to betray him, since it was not used to long walks, especially not when he was full of tobacco and drunk on cognac, he would probably have gone on walking a long time; he wanted to go somewhere far away, where he wouldn't run into anybody, least of all his own thoughts – his worries, as he called them – which followed him like a shadow. But now not even he had anywhere he could go.

The world, which perhaps just a few hours earlier he had still known how to handle, had shrunk, turned inside itself, like those empty Jewish shops and the crooked little houses on the edge of town, along with their inhabitants – mostly workers, bankrupt tradesmen, smugglers – as well as, especially, that whole phoney petit bourgeois elite, clergy included.

He had never run away from anything, nor had he ever genuinely made his confession, but he knew now that the only hell was the one inside us.

He had always used a firm hand, with his family, with his employees and even with total strangers; he knew how to handle speculators, contrabandists and black marketeers, people in whom he saw nothing but laziness and stupidity, which for him were the only true cardinal sins, and it was only in this connection that he used such terms. But most importantly, he was always strict, unsparing and firm-handed towards himself. In all respects, in both business and pleasure. He did not believe in half measures and, with regard to himself, knew no mercy, no forgiveness, no remorse.

And yet anyone who could have seen him that night would not have believed this.

Because that night something had stirred inside him, as if an unknown feeling had taken possession of him – the feeling that he was not alone in this world.

Indeed, there was a witness, even if only one, his last witness: that sign, the eye, which was with him right then and would remain with him to the very end.

For him, it had happened unexpectedly, not long before he entered the casino on the first floor of the Hotel Dobray, where József Sárdy, secretary of the Office of the Special Military Tribunal, was already waiting – the last remaining officer in the Hungarian occupying army, a man who in some perverted way still embodied the local authority, in which no one now believed and therefore people feared all the more. For they knew that a wounded beast that smells its own death is the most dangerous beast of all.

Up to then, Josip Benko had been certain that he was the only person in town able to play billiards with this degenerate ruler and win, even as he bargained, haggled and negotiated with him. Benko had such faith in his own power, prestige and crowd of debtors, that he was willing to risk anything, wager anything, so long as he got what he wanted.

At the time he had given no thought to the cost, still less to the lives that would be included in the deal. For him, it was all about the future, his own future first of all, and then everything else – the town and the region, on which he was hoping to set a price.

Now he was sitting in a corner of the abattoir, alone and in the dark. By the time he left the Hotel Dobray he knew he had been defeated, although he had not really lost anything. But it wasn't just about billiards. He had walked a long time, circling the sleepy town, looking for any of the numerous cellar dives that served liquor without a license, but no one would let him in – it was as though these small-time smugglers, petty drunks and lumpenproletariat had turned their backs on him. He realized that by now even they knew it would all soon end. They had been told that things would be different. There would be no more upper class, and all the wealth would be divided among them, the workers, as they now proudly called themselves.

But Benko hadn't cared about any of that tonight; he had just wanted to drink.

In the dull, faint light, which seemed not so much to be coming through the high windows as trapped in the abattoir, the shiny new equipment was gleaming – only today had the final touches been made and now it was fully prepared for the slaughter, butchering and packaging of horsemeat. In the morning, they would start it up for the first time.

But right now not even horses, which had been obsessing him for months, were in his thoughts.

He was drinking the Goričko *palinka* that Ruslanov regularly left in a hidden spot for the butchers, so they could warm themselves a little, forget a little, as they plunged in their knives.

Josip Benko, too, large-scale industrialist, former mayor of Sóbota, former member of parliament, and esteemed citizen, now needed to warm himself a little, to forget a little, as his mind kept returning to what Sugar Neni had told him, words meant for his ears alone.

It had happened in the corridor upstairs, in front of the door to the casino. She had stepped out of her room and motioned to him with her hand, silently. The forefinger of her left hand was pressed to her lips. Laci had told him about the incident with the pistol that morning, so Benko thought it must be about that. They went into her room. She stood there, looking old and sick – in all these years, he had never before seen her like that. Then she whispered as she pressed some papers into his hand: 'It's all here. May God help us.'

So now he had two letters.

Outside, somewhere on the very edge of this forgotten *varaš*, hidden on the plain, there was booming and cracking and flashes of light. As hard as it might be to believe, now not even this could frighten or even distract him.

Morning was still far away, and Benko was reading.

35

The crack of a billiard ball striking a man's head was all that still echoed in her ears. She was running through the cold night towards Črnske Meje, where she was long overdue. For her, she knew, this was the only way back.

On her knees in the mud, bending over the unmoving body, which she barely recognized, she had seriously thought about running away. She had money and knew where the boatmen hid, who could take her across, even down, the river; or if she was lucky, she might find someone who for good money would risk going up it, against the current, to Austria, where so many now were fleeing, although she wasn't sure why.

She had even thought then about paying with her body, offering it to anyone brave enough to go with her.

But (and this was the second time it occurred to her on this journey) she had promised to get her Kolosváry out of that hotel. And now it would be insane to go back alone across the open field.

Something told her that if anyone discovered what she had done, she would certainly be sent to jail, either by the Hungarians, who were in a hurry to leave town, or by the ones who were waiting to seize power, maybe as early as tomorrow. They would all see her as guilty: the former, because she had helped the latter; the latter, because she had worked for the former.

To top it all, she would lose Kolosváry, who was, for both sides, just another dead soldier, and dead soldiers weren't even being counted any more.

And who would believe a girlie from that filthy Hotel Dobray? What was her word against theirs?

So she needed to get back any way she could, before everything was over and they started, once again, racking the balls in some new configuration.

For she suspected that people were right who said that once the slaughter ended not only would the players change, but the cue sticks would, too, although she didn't really understand what that meant.

But still, wasn't it Linna who first started playing outside the rules? And was this just the opening shot, or had the black ball been sunk?

She felt like she had won, that she was the only one left on the green table, but also like she had fallen into a pocket from which no one could ever retrieve her.

She was fast approaching the woods, which were darker than the darkness of the night. She stopped, almost tripping over her feet. She needed to collect herself; she couldn't be seen like this in front of others, even if none of them knew who she was, even if it was still raining and the mud was clinging to her soul.

Her mouth was full of the sticky, earthy taste of death, which she could neither swallow nor wash out in the rain.

She was barefoot, without stockings, which in the face of such power and might had literally fallen from her body like the skin of a sinner. Her feet and knees were swollen – from walking, from being hit, from the hand that had tried to break her bones.

She wrapped her arms around her body. Her chest was burning; there, where the barrel of the revolver had stabbed her, she felt air seeping out, as if the wind was blowing through her, or maybe it was just blood flowing from somewhere else or maybe that invisible eye was weeping inside her, the eye – she had heard people say – through which one's conscience speaks.

That last pair of high-heeled suede shoes, borrowed no less, she had lost somewhere on the plain, or maybe she had left them near the postman, the man she had struck, who was now lying in the mud.

She was sure it was the postman, who had carried her on his bicycle from the Hotel Dobray.

Again she heard those words: 'Who are you?'

But she didn't know.

She took off the coat she was wearing and tossed it aside; it was ruined anyway. The black lambswool on the collar had fallen off, God only knew where. Swallowed by the earth, she was sure.

Everything that was lost, the shoes and the coat, she was sure she'd find a way to explain to Sugar Neni. They were close, she felt, she and this woman – closer than she would ever know.

She washed her hands in the rain and rinsed off her face; then she smoothed down her cardigan, which, amazingly, had remained unsoiled beneath the overcoat.

Again she was clean, before herself and the world, which, however, had not thought about such things in a long time.

Then she vanished into the trees.

Dear Mr Benko

your the only one that'll understand. My Linna and me – we have always been good to you. This girl of mine – she really is just mine you know. I gave her birth and I can't hide her not before myself or before God Who is my Witness. But she don't know that and my only wish is she don't find out so long as I'm alive.

I'm telling you all this cause I know every thing here is over. I'm asking you like I never askt for money which you were always so kind to give me – I'm begging you to help me – please get my daughter outa here. Somewhere faraway. For me it's over. I'll be leaving with my Jožef and his poor feet. He's all I got left in the world. I can't stay here no more cause everybody's saying it'll be difrent from now on. Ain't no place left for me here now. And my little Linna too she can't live here no more. Tho I know she's a good girl. An she can sing good too. You probly kno that youself. Only I'm afraid she's the same as her father, may his Jewish God help him even if he lost Him.

Linna's father rote me lotsa times to say he'd take her. And you dear Sir your the only one who can get her to him in Austria. He's a good man only he's always took better care of other's then of hisself and then it all turned out the way it did.

So I'm begging you with all your good will and good heart.

Yours truly,
Sugar Neni.

PS. I'm leaving you his letter's.

District Committee
Liberation Front for Prekmurje
Murska Sobota
March 25, 1945

Comrade Benko!

Contrary to your expectations and intentions, the World War is coming to its close in favour of our Western Allies and the victorious Red Army. The brave liberation forces of the Red Army are already advancing on Berlin, and any day now that nest of Hitlerism will fall.

For us Prekmurians, Slovenes on this side of the Mura, who have not yet forgotten who we are and who have not been destroyed by the boot of the Arrow Cross and the Nazis, it is important that the Red Army, with the help of our LF District Committee and the illegals, who are already crossing the Mura, as well as the many volunteers who are signing up with the Partisan detachments in Goričko, Dolinsko and Ravensko, which is to say for all of us, it is extremely important that we make preparations for our common victory and the imminent assumption of power by the people at every level.

We are well acquainted with your political orientation, as well as with your selfless assistance to our people during the war, and we are also aware of your good reputation and the influence you enjoy over the humble people of Prekmurje, who are yearning to be free.

Here the poor peasants and workers wait impatiently for freedom to come, so that together with the brotherly Red Army they can build a better and brighter future for all, regardless of politics, nationality or creed. May this be our common struggle.

We call on you, in these critical days, to assist the LF committee members, who will make personal contact with you as soon as possible, and to do so to the best of your abilities. Materially as well as politically and organizationally.

Your task is to use the channels you still maintain, as we have learned, to assist in bringing to the Prekmurje region, as soon as possible, the Partisan illegal and organizer Bogdan Hrovat, known as Miha, who for some time now has been working in the underground on the other side of the Mura.

We also authorize you to discuss a peaceful transfer of power with the commander of the Occupation unit in Murska Sobota, József Sárdy, who is located at the Hotel Dobray. Your acquaintance and good connections will serve you well.

We rely on your Prekmurian conscience and the freedom-loving nature you have so often demonstrated. But we caution you: do not foolishly abuse your good reputation or the influence you enjoy among our people.

As stated, our committee members will soon make contact with you.

Your discretion and trust will be confirmed by our illegals, who by doing this risk their lives.

Death to Fascism! Freedom to the People!

36

The cart, that ship of fools, had stopped in front of the entranceway to Benko's meat factory.

The animals were agitated; the people in the passageway, squeezed against the animals' bodies, fell silent, as if spellbound by their strength. Those farmers, horse thieves and smugglers, every one of them, could feel that within these meek, obedient animals, exhausted from their labours, there still beat the pulse of nature – which they themselves had long ago drowned in despair, fear or booze. In those big eyes, which gazed from the animals' bony skulls, one could now see boundlessness, vastness and the freedom these creatures had never been given – the most elemental aspect of their breed. This opened within them like a landscape in which no human had ever set foot, like a world that did not exist.

The people were silent, with dread in their eyes. It was like an unreal dream that no word could conjure, no hand could draw – it simply was.

Not a voice, but the moan of a crushed violin and the song of weary mariners first stirred this human wretchedness, which that morning had found its way from every corner of the deserted landscape to Lendava Road. The people in the entranceway, wedged in with their horses and cattle, were more or less trapped – they could not go forward, into the abattoir yard, until the plant supervisor, Ruslanov, let them through, nor could they go back, into the road, because the road was filled with animals and the frightened, impatient people who had brought them there: they were all moving towards the entranceway, at first to get out of the snow and the cold, then because they were afraid of being too late for the sale, but now also to get away from that mad chorus, led by the fiddler on the cart.

The horses had no one commanding them and no strength left either, since God alone knew for how long and from where they had been pulling this tuneless chorus, which most resembled a strange blend of madness and misery. Indeed, nothing but inscrutable fate could have brought together that debauched ensemble of musicians and those drunken, deranged men, who wore the uniforms of some non-existent army. Their long military overcoats, unbuttoned and unbelted, were from armies that in recent days had suddenly started intermingling. On their heads were the caps of officers and workers, without insignia or rank, as if all the deserters, drunks and musicians in the world had come together under a single roof.

The wobbly cart, which only a few minutes before had been dragging a long red flag chased by dark-haired children, was like some royal procession from a bad dream. But where this apparition was processing, with raised sabres and pistols pointing into the empty sky, and mainly without any conductor, was anybody's guess.

'Davai, davai! Palinka!' resounded from the road. That awful noise, concocted out of booze, jarring music and a language no one could comprehend, was now echoing above the heads of the horses trapped in the entranceway. Ruslanov, the Russian émigré, was the first to understand that cry of outrage. He was still in the passageway, squeezed between the gypsies (as he called them) and the horses waiting to be slaughtered. But now something beneath his own leathery hide stirred; he wanted to shout, to stick out his poisoned tongue, but the blood and spirits were clotted in his throat. With bulging eyes he stared into the dazzling light that was filtering in beneath the ceiling, and with an almost animal fear in his bones he began pushing aside both people and the agitated livestock. He slowly made his way backwards towards the stairs, which led to the first floor, where his boss, the director of the meat factory, Josip Benko, was impatiently expecting him.

But before Ruslanov disappeared up the staircase, he saw horses wrenching free of the children's hands and rising up on their hind legs. For a moment, their neighing and the stomping of their hoofs drowned out the chorus in the road, as well as the children's frightened voices, which sank beneath the surface.

When the cork finally gave way under pressure, that herd at once poured mercilessly into the abattoir yard. Foaming at the mouth, the horses started charging at the butchers, who had been standing by the exit in their long filthy coats; they were knocking them to the ground and pinning them to the wall. Like a raging river, the animals spilled across the big paved yard, which was surrounded by a high wall with no way out. To the right, however, the large metal doors of the abattoir were open, and standing in front of them were the women who worked in the meat-processing section. There, inside, the light was brightest; it came from the industrial lamps, suspended from the ceiling over long concrete worktables. At this early hour (it was not yet seven in the morning), all the lights were switched on.

Terrified by the maddened livestock, the women started screaming and waving the bloody rags they had been using to clean the butchery tables.

Now, all at once, the horses, as if aware that they were utterly trapped, rose up on their hind legs and, with all their strength, wailed into the white, deaf sky, which, perhaps, was weeping with them.

37

The woods at Črnske Meje were filled with darkness; she could feel that thick, impermeable emptiness holding the trees in place so they wouldn't run away. High above her, somewhere she couldn't see, she heard the rustling of the treetops being washed in the rain. Like the trees, she was completely unable to move, as if she, too, had been placed under a spell.

The tree she was leaning against, to catch her breath, collect her thoughts and concentrate on her mission – she did not dare, and certainly did not want, to think about what she had done – this tree, now ever more tightly, was clasping her to itself.

The bark was digging into her back; her wet, loose hair was tangled in its lower branches; and even her fingers, as she tried to free herself from its embrace, were buried so deep in the damp tree-skin that she couldn't pull them out without breaking her long nails or even the fingers themselves.

She yielded but did not surrender; she acknowledged its power over her. She knew she could not defeat nature, she could only listen to it – if, of course, there was anyone here, someone who could tell her something.

Tell her, Linna, the woman from that filthy Hotel Dobray in that skulking town, which thought only of itself. Now she couldn't wait to get far away from here, away from the town, as far as she could from anywhere.

And in fact she was on the ground again. She was lying with her legs curled next to the tree, as if it had dropped her, discarded her like a neglectful mother.

Or maybe she had fallen because she didn't know how to listen. How to obey a simple command, the request of a well-intentioned mother: Wait, don't run!

A feeling of abandonment, of emptiness, stirred inside her; it was the only thing holding her in place, like these silent trees, so she wouldn't go too far away and disappear forever. It was as if there had never been any love inside her at all. She knew she had always been alone in this world, and also that she always would be.

So now she was ready to give herself to anyone who offered a hand and set her on her feet again. She would grab hold of a stranger, or an enemy, just to get out of these woods.

It was only when she was literally being pulled off the ground that she came to. She didn't know if these people crouching in the bushes had been here all the time or if they had only just arrived. In any case, now, as she stood in front of them, she felt a desire to speak, to say anything, if only to be rid of this suffocating silence.

'You are alone,' was all she heard.

She did not understand what was meant by this – the voice inside her was still speaking, still telling her that she was the loneliest, most abandoned thing in the world, someone not even these woods would accept. But how could these people know that, let alone understand it?

She said nothing, or maybe she did, she wasn't sure.

'Don't worry about her; she's clean. That one has guarantees from above,' said a person in the back, someone she never saw. He remained hidden behind a tree even after the other two revealed themselves.

She felt relieved, but also began to worry: what did 'guaranteed from above' mean? She had never heard anyone talk about her like this.

'Put these on, woman.' The order came from a man lying on the ground.

A pair of boots were tossed at her feet.

For a moment she remembered the high-heeled suede shoes lying somewhere in the field. She wondered if she should tell them that she had been wearing shoes but lost them when she was attacked. Maybe they would even help her look for them. But no.

She bent down and picked up the heavy, hobnailed army boots. She knew she would now be able to return to the town, if nothing else, well shod.

'So long as you're with us, you'll wear them even in your sleep,' that same man said with a laugh. He was standing now. And saying this, he poked her with the barrel of his rifle.

But Linna, wearing the boots, felt safer and stronger than she ever had.

'So let's go to Sóbota,' she said decisively, speaking for the first time.

38

When was the last time I sang? The thought flashed through her mind at the sight of the deserted house, as if she was suddenly homesick for a home she had maybe never had.

Linna had been raised by a poor shoemaker named Buber, a Jew from Lendava, and the eccentric woman he lived with, who dreamed of becoming a great singer one day. Although she was sure, even as a child, that they could not be her real parents, she had never been able to summon the will or courage to ask whose child she really was. Old Buber – for as long as she could remember, he had always seemed old to her – had been kind, kinder even than might have been expected, given the circumstances. She had felt safe with him, especially because he was able to protect her from the possessive and morbidly jealous Ana, as his woman was called. But there had never been any real love between the three of them.

They had always addressed each other by their names. Linna had never called them 'Mama' or 'Father'. Still, what they had in common was a bond stronger than blood. Only music could do that.

Eccentric Ana, a tormented, jealous and too often histrionic diva, who had long ago lost her public, and old Buber, always smelling of cobbler's glue and never able to shake off the odour of old shoes, shared a refined appreciation of music. With his heavyset body and knobbly fingers, Buber was a superb violinist, while Ana, as the years went by, when the voice within her should have died, was capable of ever greater things. This was no longer the voice of an aged diva on a big stage, but something entirely different, if that was even possible. She said she had discovered the silence inside herself and it was now the only way she sang; she spoke of the wind blowing through her soul. So Ana and Buber would often go early in the morning to the vineyards outside of Lendava and stand for a while on Hadik's hill, from which the finest view opened across the plain, and listen only to their own silence. Naturally, this had its effect on Linna, too, who soon started singing and dreaming of having her own coffee-house orchestra, which she'd travel with up and down Prekmurje.

Not long after Buber died – he had made himself sick, it was said, with that cheap cobbler's glue he used – Linna found a travelling roadhouse band to sing with. But they were never able to assemble a regular coffee-house orchestra – the men soon got bored of performing and either eloped with one or another much-too-young girl or quickly drank themselves into a ditch from which they never climbed out. But Linna persisted. She occasionally sang at the Crown coffee house, at least for as long as people were coming there who remembered her great talent, as they would tell her. They wanted her even when she started pushing them away, for by now it happened more and more that if she wished to be paid she had to sing to them in bed. Thus Linna, too, and much too soon, discovered the silence within herself.

She was left without a voice or a home, to which she had stopped returning. From time to time she would hear people talk about a woman, supposedly the late, great singer Ana, who would wander through the vineyards searching tirelessly for her soul. Linna herself, more than once, heard that song drifting above the town as if borne on the wind. Then she would always light a candle in the churchyard on top of the hill, where there was a lonely grave without a name, from which the finest view opened across the plain.

With the outbreak of the Second World War, everything went from bad to worse, for Linna, too. She had to leave those hills, to go across the plain on foot in pursuit of that voice, which now no one but her was interested in.

She found shelter in Hotiza, at an inn run by a Jew, where travelling bands would stop from time to time. These musicians, who played for weddings and funerals, were in those days the last people travelling on the long road between Lendava and Sóbota. It was with these rare souls, who despite war and poverty were still venturing across the plain, now when almost nobody was having music played, that Linna sang for the last time.

In April 1944, when the Germans again occupied Prekmurje, the strict racial laws also affected her. All the Jews in Hungary lost the right to work in the civil service; they were forbidden to hire Christian workers in their factories and workshops; and they were required to wear that mark of identification, the Star of David. Many saw their factories shut down and their property confiscated, while in theatres and music halls, all actors of Jewish extraction were dismissed and, as the law stated, Jewish music could no longer be performed.

The inn in Hotiza, therefore, soon found itself without guests. People had always to some degree disparaged the Jews: 'Look at those usurers!' they would say, pointing their fingers. 'All they care about is money!' And: 'Everything they have they got at our expense!' But these poor, foolish people also knew that they couldn't do without the Jews – every single one of them went to their pubs and shops and borrowed money from their banks. So now, when they saw their newly destitute and humbled neighbours, who had suddenly lost everything, many grew wings feathered with spiteful joy.

So Linna found herself back on the street. Just as she was about to disappear somewhere on the plain, she met a trumpet player who played nothing but silence at funerals. He told her that the Hotel Dobray in Sóbota was looking for 'a lady and occasional songstress', as he put it. She suspected that this might be her last chance. Nobody knew her there so she could get rid of that Jewish star, which as a Buber she was obliged to wear – but she felt that he was not her father, and her mother's grave, on which she lit candles, had no name. Also, she thought, and in a way took courage from it: *There I could sing again.*

'The Hotel Dobray,' she repeated to herself. It sounded impressive.

And so, on April 26, 1944, early in the morning, she arrived at the door of the hotel. Laci, the hotelier, who was standing on the front steps, asked her: 'Who are you?'

In Ascher's abandoned house, opposite the Hotel Dobray, everything was quiet now. The woman, still naked except for the high army boots, which she had not removed even in bed, was standing in the middle of the airless room. She held a pistol in her left hand and, without actually aiming, was pointing it somewhere in front of herself. The man with the hump – Hunchback Miha, as he had just stammered out to her – whom she had smuggled into town in the dark of night, was still crouching on all fours at her feet. 'Who are you?' – again the words echoed inside her, although she didn't know where they came from. She had had a long, wretched, sleepless night.

She had stayed awake even after the man fell asleep with his gun in his hand. But before this helpless, crippled creature began to snore, he had whispered to her, had begged her with those big childlike eyes, to sleep with him. She had laughed. She knew these men, these wounded heroes, oh God, she'd had so many of them, had comforted so many – lonely soldiers she called them – she knew them to the depths of their souls. And then, of course, he started shouting and threatening her, which was just another little game: of frustration and overwrought desire. She had stood up and showed him her breasts. 'Now be quiet, it's all yours,' she had whispered, and then slipped off that muddy dress, which just hours before, in the middle of a field under the dark, open sky, had been ripped and grabbed by exactly the same sort of hungry, craving, abandoned body.

Linna now stood naked before him, holding the pistol in her left hand, wearing only those boots, which she would never again take off. Hunchback Miha was watching her silently and, finally, when he was dragging himself towards the door, there were tears trickling down his nose.

That was when Linna, the woman from the Hotel Dobray, as people would later remember her, or maybe not, sang for the last time in her life. The earth itself seemed to be touched. That morning in late March 1945, it echoed through the streets and resonated in the souls of this sleepy *varaš*. If anyone then was looking at the sky, they would certainly have noticed that sign, the eye, as if the sky, too, was weeping along with them.

Franz Schwartz, who had been hiding in the summer house, was at the time walking towards the Sóbota synagogue, where a smouldering fire was sending smoke into the sky. He heard that singing as he looked up, or was it only the freezing children warming their hands?

39

'József Sárdy, secretary of the Office of the Special Military Tribunal' – that was how he introduced himself to people, as if he possessed a magic formula that opened every door. He had spent the whole morning wandering through the streets of Budapest, looking for that Jewish Library to which he had been summoned. But as soon as he addressed someone, reciting his name and rank in that specially ordained, raised voice, a voice he had quickly picked up from the other officials, he ran into problems. At the mention of the Jewish Library, everyone just hunched their shoulders, turned their backs and hastened on their way, as if his magic had instantly lost its power.

He was seriously tempted to abandon his search, go back to the office in the annexe, lock the door and lie low until evening, when he would again feel safe and strong, among his own kind, he thought, on the floating platforms, with women who listened to him and men who drank with him, so long as he was paying.

But what if this was a test his superiors had set up for him, he suddenly wondered; if so, there must be a solution. Yes, they were probably waiting for him there, and not just him but everyone who passed the test, and then, formally and with all due honours, they would be named secretaries of the Office of the Special Military Tribunal. And there was sure to be an excess of candidates, which meant he had better find this damned Jewish Library fast, if he didn't want to come in last. Because if that happened, he thought with alarm, then tonight he'd be drinking for the last time, with no more job and no more drinking companions.

The solution, he suspected, was just around the corner. He came upon a destitute Jew, a bird monger, selling mangy messenger pigeons.

'József,' he introduced himself casually and offered his hand. Now he thought himself even cleverer than he had previously imagined.

'What would you like?' the pigeon monger asked.

'Can you tell me where the Jewish Library is?'

'Buy this pigeon,' the man said. 'He knows the way. He used to deliver mail there.' He placed the bird on top of his head. It started cooing, as if to confirm his master's words, and settled on his cap.

'How much do you want for him?'

'This bird is worth as much as all the others put together. He's the only one who knows the way.'

József Sárdy, secretary of the Office of the Special Military Tribunal, he silently recited to himself as he weighed his options.

'I'll buy them all.'

He picked up the two cages with the pigeons and started running after the other bird, which was now flying high above the street in the direction of the Jewish Library.

A few minutes later, out of breath and covered in feathers and bird droppings, he found himself back at the very same spot where he had just bought the pigeons. He had simply run around the building. On the door was a sign which said: *Jewish Library.* The pigeon monger, of course, was nowhere to be seen.

He knew he had been well and truly swindled. Now he didn't have enough in his pocket even for a single night out. But at the moment he couldn't think about his decadent companions or even about revenge for these horrid birds. He was in a hurry to get to the meeting and feared that he really would end up last.

He entered the library. But before the heavy door shut behind him, the only free pigeon escaped, flying off in search of its wily master.

József had never seen so many books, but that was not what bothered him. He seemed to have sunk into the earth among these high shelves, which reached all the way to the ceiling, amid a silence such as he had never experienced. He would very likely have stood there a long time, without moving, had he not heard the pigeons shamelessly cooing and fluttering in their rickety cages.

It would not do, he thought, to show up for a banquet with these mangy birds. He was, after all, a secretary and should act like one; he had to think of his reputation.

This filth and shame, which he brought on himself out of ignorance, he must urgently hide somewhere. He couldn't just leave the birds here, cooing and crapping all over the place, he thought, now seized with anger, and fear as well. Again he was a child, with that same secret shame and humiliation awakening within him that had been implanted by the boys from his street because he had been the only one who had not had the courage to mutilate a bird. But now he was a man, in the entrance hall, as it were, of something big and important, which he didn't know how to explain even to his own mother.

He gritted his teeth and reached into the cages with both hands. It took just a moment until only cooing remained in the air.

Then all was silent again.

Somewhere high overhead, at the top of a twisting staircase, someone was tenderly playing a piano. Slowly, he climbed the stairs and walked down a long, narrow corridor to a room where he was sure they were expecting him.

He was amazed to discover that he wasn't too late. There were only two people in the small room, which was crammed with books, binders and stacks of folders. The one playing the piano was an older man, somewhat thin, with long fingers – he looked just like the pigeon monger who a short while earlier had shamelessly swindled him. The other, who was sitting at a desk, was impeccably groomed, with basically no distinguishing characteristics – a functionary, like any other functionary in the world.

József was initially relieved not to be last. Or maybe, he thought, it really was just him they were expecting. Which meant, he then thought, it really was some strictly official business matter; so it wasn't a banquet.

'Sit down,' the clerk told him.

'I don't mind standing. I've been sitting for entire days in the office, you know.'

'There,' the man insisted, pointing to a chair with his pencil.

'So, József,' he continued, checking a long list of names.

'József Sárdy, secretary of the Office of the Special Military Tribunal,' József said.

'Hungary has endorsed the final solution, but she hasn't yet done anything about it,' the man said.

'That's very nice music. They don't play music like that any more on the river.'

'You leave tonight, as you requested.'

'Tonight? Where I am going?'

'Far away. There, too, there is much that needs to be done.'

'Yes?'

'There are birds that need to be cleaned and put into cages, if you understand my meaning. The final solution to the Jewish question is our priority now. Here are your official orders. Look them over and leave them with the doorman.'

'Downstairs?'

'Now go! You're the last one!'

'Eichmann!' he stammered, when he glanced at the signature on the document, which he did not completely understand.

'Now go! And as for you, keep playing!' the clerk said, abruptly ending the conversation.

József Sárdy, secretary of the Office of the Special Military Tribunal, left on the night train from Budapest for some distant unknown province at the very edge of his great homeland, to a world bounded by the Raba and Mura rivers, which was all he could understand from the map; everything else was a mystery to him.

For the first time he was wearing a proper military uniform and an officer's high boots – he thought it all extremely grand. He received his pistol the next morning in Szentgotthárd, where he joined up with the German troops marching to Prekmurje.

The first trip József ever took was spoiled only by the rain, which fell day and night. He did not remove his damp, muddy officer's boots, which he was not yet used to wearing, until the final stop. He felt his feet swelling and the blisters burning him, but again he just gritted his teeth, because how could he take his boots off in front of rank-and-file soldiers?

They crossed the Raba, and then struck up a long, fast march to Sóbota, which was led by the Germans.

They arrived in the town on April 16, 1944, towards evening. They moved into the vacated rooms of the Sóbota school and that very night assumed command of the town. At once they imposed strict racial laws, which the local Jews, whose numbers were not small, accepted quietly, though not without grumbling. In the days that followed, they shut down twenty-six businesses and workshops. On April 26, 1944, at exactly five o'clock in the afternoon,

József Sárdy, secretary of the Office of the Special Military Tribunal, moved into the Hotel Dobray, where he was given his own office. Later, the Germans assigned him a small defence unit, which was constantly at his disposal.

It was all a modest reward for what he would accomplish over the next few days here. He was sure that someone in Budapest was thinking of him.

Even before inspecting his new quarters, he stepped out onto the balcony above the entrance to the Hotel Dobray, where, for the first time in his life, he had the view he could only dream of before. Calmly, he looked at the well-dressed concert-goers, who were still standing below. They were Jews, he realized when he saw that nearly every one of them was wearing a big star-shaped patch; then, right in front of his nose, a pigeon fluttered its wings. He was about to reach for his pistol but restrained himself: he mustn't frighten the birds below, pressed against the wall of the hotel. Another moment (he checked his watch), and the lorries would be here.

And now, eleven months later, in late March 1945, he was still here, at the Hotel Dobray. He was preparing for one last game of billiards. The woman, who for him was still nameless, lay on the table in front of him.

40

The shot from a light officer's pistol was fired a few minutes before seven in the morning. A mare, one who had been fighting a long time, neighing and standing on her hind legs, who had kicked two of the foremen and bitten one of the butchers, now fell onto her forelegs and lay wounded in the abattoir yard. She was wheezing and drooling. Then some butchers grabbed her neck to hold her down; they watched as Ruslanov, the supervisor, foaming with fury, walked up and shot her one more time.

The startled horses, trapped in the entranceway of the Benko meat-processing plant, went wild. They were jumping and biting people and animals, until finally they cleared a path to the street. Then they rushed into Lendava Road and down towards Main Square, opposite the Hotel Dobray.

The frenzied herd pulled with it the cart with the inebriated Russian officers, who had arrived in town too early, bringing the musicians with them – the bulk of the Red Army was still making its way towards Sóbota. This lost troop had been up all night drinking *palinka* on Lake Bukovnica; as morning approached, they had a desire to ride in a horse-drawn vehicle, so they piled into a cart and had themselves driven across the plain. Naturally, the young fiddler who was supposed to drive the cart did not have the courage to object. To quell his fear, he started drinking with the Russians and let the horses take them to Sóbota – it was the only route they knew.

They made their first stop just as day was breaking. Fog lay on the fields near Rimska Čarda, and a fine snow was falling. The drunken soldiers, chilled to the bone – they had been lying in the cart in only their shirtsleeves – now leapt to the ground. All that could be heard in the distance were the last crows, which would soon be flying away. The men, half asleep, were relieving themselves around the cart and laughing, at God knows what. But before they had all clambered back on, one of them, a man who couldn't stop hiccupping, croaked out: 'Germans!' – although he wasn't entirely sure it wasn't a mirage.

As if sobering up at once, the men grabbed their rifles and pistols (one picked up his sabre) and prepared their weapons. They had no idea what they were aiming at, but they were ready to do battle. The soldier with the sabre stood up and shouted: 'Go! Go!'

The shapes moving through the field like shadows or a mirage, only a stone's throw from the road on which that ship of fools was sailing, stopped for a moment when they saw the danger, but before they could all get down and hide on the ground, a shot rang out.

The soldier with the sabre jumped off the cart and staggered over to the person lying on the ground. Without knowing why, he dragged him to the road and they loaded him on the cart. He was wearing a long overcoat with no insignia. A deserter, they all agreed. Only a few hours later, Franz Schwartz would identify the man in the entranceway of the Benko meat-processing plant.

When the cart was again trundling down the road towards Sóbota, the shadows started rising from the earth – these were the gypsy children who had been following Ascher, perhaps the entire night, or maybe these living children were escorting him into town, after he had spent the night by one of their hidden fires; he must have promised them money if they could get him home safely.

Now the children were running, tripping and chasing after that wobbly cart, in which their benefactor lay dead. But they knew that a dead benefactor was better than none, for his people, if he had any, would reward them simply for bringing him back to them. Sorrow and joy have their price, as people here were known to say – getting buried and getting married both take money.

The confused, frightened soldiers, who had kept watch through the night by the windows of the Hotel Dobray, at first merely stared in silence at the herd of maddened horses stampeding towards them across Main Square.

It was not until Private Kolosváry fell, who had stood defence-less at the window thinking of his carved horses, that they too began firing. Trapped in the crossfire, the horses, whether struck or grazed or simply petrified, were falling in the street and on the square.

The astonished Russians were shooting blindly from their wobbly cart, which was racing down the street out of control. They didn't come to their senses until they suddenly found themselves under fire from the Hotel Dobray; as fast as they could they leapt from the cart and ran among the houses, where for the next few days they received board and lodging.

Although the Germans were not prepared to defend the town, a few days later, on April 2, they blew up the bridge over the Ledava River at the end of Lendava Road.

The Red Army liberated Sóbota on April 3, 1945.

Later that morning, towards the end of March 1945, there was a second when everything went quiet, as if for a moment everybody was looking up at the sky.

The silence that then permeated the souls in this forgotten *varaš* can, perhaps, still be felt today; sometimes it sounds like a forgotten melody, borne on the wind through the streets – and this wind truly is the last evidence, the only witness, that a secret once lingered in this region but then had to flee; even so, people here are known to say that more and more – like the tolling of bells, warning them – they hear as a distant echo the neighing of horses.

The Great
Pannonian Music

It happened once upon a time, a long time ago, but not so long ago that nobody would remember any more. In one of those small towns – a *varaš*, as the townsfolk called it, similar to hundreds of other anonymous towns scattered across the Pannonian lowland, where strangers only rarely visit.

The dusty road that leads to this invisible place is hidden by tall poplars. So traveller, remember: when you see a line of trees in the distance, recall the story you once heard, or perhaps read. Because now that you know, you must pass it on, so it is never forgotten.

The town, then, was peacefully living its life and keeping its secrets somewhere in the middle of the great plain, hidden in a pocket of land between the Mura and Raba rivers.

Here people were still known to say, or it might simply slip out of them, that they believed in souls. Maybe that was just a legend, preserved as nothing more than a beautiful thought, which had got caught in their hearts and spoke to them there. Sometimes a person has to listen to this inner voice, just as a person has to love somebody.

At this late hour only a few lamps were still burning in the little windows of the squat houses, which appeared to be dozing beneath their crooked roofs. The dusty, winding streets, too, above which naked light bulbs swayed in a gentle breeze, appeared to be deserted. For as soon as it grew dark, people would sit by the stove and quietly converse. Bitter words revolved around the war, fear and the deprivations that had affected all the people who lived in this world. For somewhere outside the warm houses and beyond the walls of the gardens, where children were still playing, rumblings and explosions were heard, maybe even weeping. In other words, in those flashes of light on the horizon at night, when the earth itself shook, everyone felt fear and the nearness of death, which they preferred not to talk about in front of the children.

The adults, of course, were worried; they were afraid. Mothers and fathers, grandfathers, grandmothers, uncles – they knew that the children saw and felt their fear, but not many could find the right words to describe their distress. The easiest way for them to tell the children was to hold them close, sit them on their laps and whisper: 'We love you.'

So it was once upon a time and so it should be today, too.

1

Edina was sitting in the corner behind the stove, carefully winding yarn onto wooden spools in the dim light. In this way she would help her father every evening as he pushed the pedals on the sewing machine beneath the only lamp in the room. Hunched over and saying few words, he worked long into the night, sewing men's suits and women's dresses, mending overcoats and patching children's shirts. They were alone in the little room. Edina's mother had been tired and was already lying in bed; in near darkness, she was reading a thick book with black covers. She would often interrupt her reading to calmly make some remark or observation, or tell her husband something, and only then would he stop pedalling the sewing machine and reply: 'That's beautiful. Yes, they really know how to live over there,' adding: 'When there's finally peace here, we'll have to take our Edina for a visit.' The girl, of course, their one and only love, was not yet able to understand everything they said. But she did not ask many questions either; she trusted whatever her mother and father told her. She believed that the great bloodshed would soon end – that is what she heard the grownups saying, who, however, were coming by less often than before. Then, maybe, they really would go there, to where all the beauty described in books could be found.

What Edina was now able to understand and decipher from her mother's and father's words was that whenever they spoke about true beauty, they were actually thinking of something else, which, to be sure, was closely related to the beauty of a flower, a picture, music or the starry sky.

Now, when she heard the word *beauty*, Edina felt warmth, peace and the love of her parents. It had always been like that in her family, even when they did not talk about beauty.

With this thought, and with the long yarn in her hands, Edina was about to doze off when somebody rapped gently on the outside blinds. It made a pleasant jingling in the room, as if angels were passing through – she had learned quite a lot about angels from books, but so far she had seen them only in her imagination.

Edina looked up slowly, her eyes sparkling, as if she was still thinking about something beautiful, maybe trying for a moment to again imagine her guardian angel, with whom she would often chat in her thoughts, as she had been doing earlier, in the late afternoon. She saw her father, who had stopped the sewing machine, take the paraffin lamp down from the wall; he looked puzzled. He carefully reduced the flame so he could more easily look through the blinds into the darkness.

'Who on earth could be out at this hour?' her mother asked in a loud voice, as she shut her heavy book with a snap.

'Nothing to worry about. It's Mr Schwartz,' her father said soothingly, and went to open the back door that led to the courtyard.

Although it was not yet nine o'clock, it was still dangerous to be out in the street knocking on people's front doors in the evening. Hungarian sentries patrolled the major roads at night, and when they saw somebody in the street, they would demand to see identification and thoroughly examine the person, who would then often be hauled off to prison for interrogation.

Edina, now fully alert, was secretly delighted by this late and unexpected visit.

Mr Schwartz was a shopkeeper. By birth a Jew from the town of Čakovec, he had moved here many years earlier, before Edina was born, after he married a Sóbota woman. His little general store, where he lived above the shop with his family, was not very far from Edina's house.

In the period before the Second World War, there were many such shops in the town; they sold general household goods or textiles, and most of them were owned by Jews. In Prekmurje, in fact, the Jews formed an important and numerous community, which enjoyed prestige and helped to shape the day-to-day life of Sóbota, which was rapidly developing into an exemplary middle-class town.

From time to time, and especially before the holidays, her mother would send Edina to Schwartz's shop for a bag of sugar, so she knew the gentleman by sight. But she had only a vague memory of the narrow shop with its wooden shelves, which were stacked to the ceiling with boxes.

The shopkeeper would reach these wares with the help of a ladder, and then, in front of each and every customer, he would read out the carefully inscribed labels on the fronts of the boxes, as if he was boasting about the hidden riches this tiny general store contained.

'Sugar, saccharine, flour (both corn and white), matches, lamp oil, eggs, cigarettes, sweets …' – and on and on until at last he pulled the desired box off the shelf. Then, skilfully, he would place this big box on the tall counter and, with a slight smile, open it in front of the customer's curious eyes. A moment's pause, and then he would look at the customer from behind his round spectacles and quickly ask:

'Perhaps you would like something sweet, too?'

And, of course, the poor but enchanted woman and child who were standing in front of him would have to think. Again their eyes would dart across those mysterious boxes, in which such desirable things were hidden, as the shopkeeper's friendly words about their contents continued to echo somewhere in their heads. Then, with great pleasure and almost childish enthusiasm, Mr Schwartz would again begin to recite:

'Maybe a jar of excellent honey – look, here's some acacia honey, as sweet as the sun – or maybe a local wildflower honey, from an excellent beekeeper in Goričko; no need to worry, I know the gentleman personally,' he would say as he lifted the jar of thick, reddish goodness towards the light. 'Or what's this here?' he would whisper with a sideways glance as he brought out a pretty little box from beneath the counter. 'Just for you,' he would add, 'Turkish delight, made with almonds and walnuts – the real thing. I tell you, there's nothing better for these cold days. For a long time to come, whenever you think of this treat, you'll find yourself missing the winter. I tell you, those Turks really knew how to live.'

'Well, all right,' almost everyone then said, 'we'll take something for the holidays, too.' Of course, that was mostly in better times, as they called the years before the war, which, overnight, had robbed them of life's small delights.

It had been a long time since Edina had visited Schwartz's shop; there was never enough money in the house. Her father was getting fewer and fewer orders, and the ones he did get were mainly for repairs and adjustments – patching, shortening or lengthening dresses and suits – not enough to make a living from. Now even the town's finest families, who continued to frequent the coffee houses, had stopped having clothes made to order. The deprivations, poverty and especially the despondency brought by the war had taken their toll on everyone.

The girl was, however, much better acquainted with the large, well-tended garden behind the shopkeeper's house, in the middle of which stood a fine white-painted summer house. Every spring, the first ripe cherries would appear on a tree by the low garden wall, bringing smiles to the faces of children far and wide. And it didn't stop at smiles, of course. Edina herself had often partaken of that forbidden fruit, pilfered by the boys in her street.

But her conscience was clear as she waited for the shopkeeper to enter: the cherries were not yet ripe, so Mr Schwartz had not come to complain to her father about some innocent theft.

'Shalom, good evening,' Mr Schwartz greeted them amiably as he stepped into the warm, narrow little room. 'Forgive me for disturbing you at such a late hour,' he continued, 'but my son, Izak, had a long practice tonight with his teacher, who will unfortunately be leaving soon.'

'Well, please, have a seat, both of you. Tell me what I can do for you,' her father replied; he had sat down again at the sewing machine.

Edina saw how he was fidgeting with the long measuring tape, which almost certainly meant he felt a bit embarrassed. The late visit had surprised him. It had been a while since he had welcomed such a fine customer, which is how he normally described it when a well-respected gentleman of means came to see him. He was always a little flustered at first, talking either too much or not at all, but he would quickly regain his composure. He knew he could handle any order, no matter how difficult. He was thoroughly familiar with the stylish cuts and fabrics that were then in fashion. If anything went wrong, his wife would help him: she was glad to drop by one of the better Jewish clothing stores, where all the styles were on display. She would take a good look at the garments and then make a full report to her husband. Of course, she particularly enjoyed going to a coffee house and looking through the foreign, mostly German, fashion magazines, which also featured plenty of sewing patterns.

So, then, one could have anything custom-made at the Šiftar Tailoring Salon, or as people said more simply, at Géza the tailor's.

But the girl was now unable to concentrate on the conversation between her father and the shopkeeper. Her dreaming eyes had been awakened by the boy, who was standing silently next to the table and leaning against the stove. Edina, a little shyly but not timidly, watched him out of the corner of her eye, in the semi-darkness, in which the boy's shape was now the only thing gleaming.

She couldn't help staring at his soft, gentle face, which was distinguished by a sharp masculine nose and, especially, those dark, deep eyes.

When the boy looked in her direction, also shyly, as if he could feel the girl watching him, for a moment she couldn't breathe. It was as if she had been touched by something powerful, something she had never yet seen; and, in fact, she would never be able to describe this feeling. She thought: 'If angels do exist somewhere, then he must certainly be like them.'

But a moment later the boy lowered his eyes. She saw the flush on his otherwise pale, serious cheek, and then his long and shaggy black hair, which told her unmistakably that he was still not much more than a child. Finally, Edina's eyes rested on the boy's simple cap, the kind worn by all the Jewish boys in town. Their fathers, however, always wore brimmed hats, as Mr Schwartz was wearing now.

In the eyes of the townspeople, these black caps and hats were a sign of the separateness and secretiveness of the Jews, as well as, more often than not, an object of ridicule.

Perhaps that was what the boy sensed in the girl's eyes when he abruptly stepped to the table and sat down next to his father. For he must have been familiar with – must have often had to bear, helplessly – the mockery and needless envy of the other children in town, which is why he never liked spending time with them.

Edina, too, sensed that something had hurt the boy's feelings. And again she retreated inside herself, as if ashamed. She picked up some yarn and, distractedly, started to wind it on a wooden spool.

'This is for Mrs Šiftar,' the shopkeeper said, placing a small package on the table.

'Thank you, but that wasn't necessary.' Her father was surprised.

'It's coffee. Genuine Brazilian.'

'Oh my! I doubt we even remember what it smells like.' Then, a little cautiously, he asked, 'And what can we do for you?' The tailor guessed it was something important, maybe so important he wouldn't be able to do it.

'Well, it's like this,' Mr Schwartz began, taking the boy by the arm as he continued: 'In ten days, on the twenty-sixth of April, my son, Izak, will have his bar mitzvah – he'll be thirteen years old. That's a big celebration for us,' the father said, clasping his son's arm even more tightly. 'And on this same day he will perform his first concert – at the Dobray coffee house,' he concluded, immensely proud.

At the shopkeeper's confident words, so full of joy and uncon-cealed love, the girl again lowered the yarn to her lap. But now she couldn't catch the boy's eyes, which were staring fixedly at the ceiling. She suspected he was avoiding her; maybe he really was offended, or maybe he was just moved and uplifted by his father's words.

'That will be a big day for your family! Please, tell me if there is something I can do to see that the boy is nicely attired,' her father replied. He knew what he would be asked to do.

'Certainly, Mr Šiftar. My wife and I are counting on your diligent hand, and also on your discretion. I'll be frank. Izak needs a suit for the concert. And as I'm sure you'll understand, these are difficult times for us, too. We have less and less merchandise to sell and, mainly, fewer and fewer customers to sell it to. We ourselves have had to sell – to loan sharks and war profiteers – everything we have of value in our home, bit by bit. If the bloodshed doesn't end soon, we'll have to barter even our most sacred things for a chicken.

'So I am asking you, Mr Šiftar, here is my best black suit – remove the stitches and make it into something nice for my son. If need be, my wife will give you her best coat, too, just so long as you make him a decent suit.'

That is what Mr Schwartz, the respected Sóbota shopkeeper, said that evening. Géza the tailor was the only person, right then, who understood his distress, and his pride as well, for he sensed that, in deprivation, suffering and pain, people are more alike than at any other time.

The tailor took the boy's measurements and promised the shopkeeper that the suit would look new. And that he should tell his wife not to worry: she would not be cold next winter. There would be no need to cut up her coat.

Over the next few days Edina, at first, felt like she was bored. The weather had turned bad again; it was always raining or drizzling, and in the evening a sharp, silky wind whipped around the corners. The birds she had been so looking forward to seeing were staying away from the rooftops in town. Yet just the day before she had seen the first spring birds returning to the area, which meant that the nest beneath the eaves of their house would soon be full of life again. And she would again be waking up to beautiful birdsong.

But now winter, which had been on its way out, was once more baring its teeth. Her mother, wishing of course to console her, to cheer her up, said: 'Sometimes in April it even snows.' She had noticed the girl's low spirits and irritability; at every pleasant word from her or her husband, their daughter said only: 'Oh, leave me alone.'

Those evenings were forgotten when she would sit in her father's workroom and amuse herself with the colourful buttons and threads. She might still sit in her usual corner, but she didn't touch the sewing things. She just stared at the ceiling, as if she was copying the boy whose suit her father was making. Naturally, she was only interested in when Mr Schwartz and his son, the boy who was about to give his first concert, would be coming by for the fitting. More than once, secretly, so her father wouldn't yell at her, she had taken the unfinished suit in her hands. She could easily imagine how splendid the young man would look in this black suit, standing with his violin in front of the audience in the coffee house. 'Oh, if only I could be there,' she silently wished. But that really was just a dream, for who would ever invite her to the Dobray coffee house – Edina, a little girl, the daughter of a tailor from the edge of town – to a concert no less! Only fine gentlemen and their wives would be there, and maybe unmarried young people, too, boys and girls who were already adults, and of course schoolteachers, clergymen, respected shop owners and local artists – everyone who mattered.

School had been unexpectedly cancelled that week.

On Monday morning, even before her teacher, Miss Ilonka, could hand out the tablets and chalk to the children, their much-hated, much-feared headmaster, Mr Kálmán Paál, accompanied by a few of the Hungarian soldiers who had occupied the school, appeared before the children and delivered a brief but sombre speech:

'School will be closed for the foreseeable future. In Sóbota, and in the entire region under the Hungarian state, the leadership is being replaced. In glorious Budapest, the government of Miklós Kállay has resigned in shame. Our new president, Döme Sztójay, has assumed power and, with our German troops, will defend our beloved Hungarian land. As headmaster of this important institution, I am obliged to respect the new authority, and so, until the order is reversed, school will be closed. We must each of us do our part to defend great Hungary from the Bolsheviks and the Western aggressors, especially the Americans, who have no respect for land, God or king. Now everyone go home and remain there until further notice.'

Although Headmaster Kálmán Paál had, unusually, spoken to the students in Slovene, which gave his words an even sharper edge, the children did not understand much of what he said.

It was indeed strange that Paál had not spoken in Hungarian on this occasion. Although he was himself a Slovene, and was born in Sóbota, in his heart he was devoted to Hungary, even if it was the occupier. At school, in the street and very likely even at home, he spoke exclusively in that foreign tongue. Miss Ilonka, too, who unlike the headmaster was a native Hungarian (she had been transferred here from Szombathely), also, naturally, spoke to her students in Hungarian. So, although the children regularly attended school, they did not learn very much, for they did not understand the language.

In any case, what they understood now, at the very least, was that they had to go home at once, each to their own house, with no poking about in the street or wandering into alleyways, where they would usually play for a while before scattering in all directions.

2

On Friday, Edina was awakened by a sunbeam playing on her sleepy eyes. At first she thought somebody was teasing her with a singing blade of grass. She had a tickle in her nose and tried to hide under the covers, but her curiosity soon got the better of her.

She peeked out at the world and felt like a flower that had just blossomed. She opened her eyes wide and inhaled. After a week of fog and rain their little house was again full of sunshine. From the front room, where even at this early hour her father's sewing machine would normally be humming, came the smell of genuine coffee. The girl, of course, at once thought of the boy with the violin and his black suit, which very possibly was now finished.

It was still only morning but already she felt that today could be a happy day.

Her parents were sitting by the window, quietly sipping their coffee. When the girl saw them, they seemed to be glowing in the sunshine. She knew they were enjoying the coffee, which they had not been able to allow themselves in a long time. All they ever had in the house was that bitter barley coffee, which they drank without sugar because they were trying to save money on that, too.

'But still,' Edina thought as she looked at them, 'there must be something else between them, between us – something more, which others will never have. Maybe it's love.'

Edina could feel it. She had known love since the day she was born. Now, when it was just the three of them in this little room, bathed in sunlight, and the first spring swallows would almost certainly be returning to the eaves, she knew that this was, perhaps, beauty in its entirety.

She felt safe, even though outside – just beyond their door, one might say – war was raging, and in the coming days would bare its murderous teeth in Sóbota. But this was all somewhere else now, far from her eyes, far from her heart.

Before she had even sat down at the table and drunk her milk, her father said to her: 'The sun is shining and the suit is ready to be fitted. Go to Mr Schwartz's house and tell him that he and his son may come by this evening.'

The girl's eyes again lit up. She was happy and sad at the same time. Something was telling her, as if she only now suspected it, that she would be here, in this little house she loved, beside her father's sewing machine and her mother's books, for a long time to come, but even so, she was already saying goodbye. Although she did not yet fully understand this, she said 'thank you' as if wanting to thank them for what they had given her, something no one could ever measure or weigh. That was it – that something more.

The sun had already risen above the town. The low, squat houses of the local tradesmen, pressed one against the other like pigeons beneath the eaves, had been washed in the rain. Their white façades were gleaming in the sharp light. The large gardens behind the houses had turned green, as if overnight the wind had breathed life into nature. This was normally the time of year when people would emerge from their houses after the long winter and start working in their gardens. They would prune the vines and fruit trees, rake the grass and dig beds for vegetables and flowers.

But not a living soul was in sight, as if everyone was still hibernating with the bears. The yards and the dusty narrow lanes between the houses were empty. Not even the birds Edina had been so looking forward to seeing were anywhere about.

Schwartz's shop stood in a row of tall, two-storey buildings on Flower Street, a long, broad thoroughfare. Edina lived in a low little house, one of the many houses hidden behind the fine homes and shops of the town's elite. The location of a person's house, whether it was on one of the main roads or out of sight, among the gardens, was yet another way people decided, and could tell, just who was who in Sóbota. Shopkeepers, lawyers and doctors lived in two-storey houses, looking on to an important street, while tailors, butchers, shoemakers, blacksmiths, printers and everyone else lived behind them, in an invisible shadow.

There was a shortcut to Schwartz's shop, by a lane that ran between the garden walls and through a narrow passage between some houses; it usually took the girl less than ten minutes. But today, surprisingly, she was not in any hurry. A new world seemed to have suddenly opened inside her. She was admiring the town, which in the sunlight offered itself to her newly awakened eyes. She felt she was seeing it for the first time.

She was stopping in front of window displays, and every so often, with no particular intention or desire, would linger over the watches and hats, the sweets and bicycles. Although she knew she was not supposed to wander through the town by herself, especially not on the main roads, because: 'My darling child, there's a war going on. You can't understand this yet but something bad could happen to you,' her father had warned her. And even the hated headmaster, Kálmán Paál, had drummed it into their heads that they must stay close to home, as far away as possible from the streets and courtyards.

That whole week, which she had spent at home because the school was closed, she had sensed that something bad was being planned and plotted. Everyone had been whispering, more and more, about how the Germans and Hitler's army, when they marched into town, would certainly be sowing death.

Although the people of Sóbota had known the horror of war ever since the first German occupation, which ended on April 16, 1941, when the town passed into the administration of the Hungarian military, they were genuinely afraid of the new German occupation. It had been exactly three years since the Nazis' departure, and now they had come back. There was this, too: it was five days until the Schwartz boy's concert. Maybe a coincidence, or maybe not.

But Edina was now full of entirely different thoughts. There was music in her heart, a music she had not yet heard.

People say that dreams always come true, but you have to believe in them. That may have been just what the girl was thinking, or perhaps, at that moment, she was not thinking anything, but only reading:

All are Invited to Attend the Debut Concert of
IZAK SCHWARTZ
Violin and Orchestra

Hotel Dobray, Sobota
April 26, 1944, at 5 p.m.

The concert will be followed by a reception and a collection for renovations to the Sobota surgical department

The poster was hanging in the window of Mayer's Shoe Boutique. Now, of course, Edina's heart was fluttering. Her imagination, which she could barely contain at the best of times, again took flight.

She saw herself in the coffee house, which was filled with well-mannered townspeople, all of them enthralled by the young violinist's virtuoso performance; they were standing in a long queue to shake his hand. She, too, was standing in the queue, of course, holding a flower in her hand. Slowly she moved towards the boy in the black suit, who had his bow and violin clutched beneath his arm. Soon they would look into each other's eyes. She was sure he would recognize her in the crowd. Now, certainly, he would step down from the stage and offer her his hand. From the excitement and the music, which was still singing to her, she would squeeze the rose so tightly her palm would start to bleed. Only another step or two …

Who knows how long the girl would have continued daydreaming if she had not been startled by the rumble of lorries and a column of soldiers in black helmets, marching through town down the dusty street. At the sight of these fully armed troops and the big flag with the swastika, Edina's blood froze. She had heard about such things from people's talk, as well as from soldiers returning from the front, but she had never actually seen them. She was seized by a fear she had never felt before, a fear she would never forget.

She ran as fast as she could away from the street and did not stop until she was standing among the gardens of her own neighbourhood, thinking that she was safe here, among the little houses she knew. This was her world – small, warm and guarded by an invisible shadow.

She was already intending to run home and hide with her mother and father, who by now would be getting worried, wondering why she was taking so long. But still, she really did want to see the boy that evening wearing his new suit. So she would have to go as fast as possible to Schwartz's shop and back again, before her father went out looking for her.

She was still catching her breath from the fear she had felt just a little earlier. But she was determined to deliver her father's message. She wanted to see the boy, even if, perhaps, she couldn't admit that to herself. This was her first time, and she had no way of knowing. So we need to forgive her.

She ran there, this time taking the shortcut.

The first thing she noticed was the cherry tree, all white with blossom. Then she heard the violin: it was singing, as only springtime can sing. She could barely curb the sound of her footsteps, her breathing; she was afraid of disturbing that music, of scaring off the angels. At once, she forgot the soldiers, the swastika and the fear they had inspired in her. She was entranced, more entranced than she could ever be by even the most beautiful watches, hats, sweets or bicycles.

She walked on tiptoe beneath the blossoming cherry and hid by the low wall that surrounded the shopkeeper's garden. The wind was carrying, was twirling, the music and the tiny white petals from the tree and scattering them across the houses and down the streets. Perhaps the music that day drowned out even the thunder of artillery fire and the marching of army boots, and not just here, in this small *varaš*, this quiet region, but on all battlefronts around the world, wherever blood was still flowing.

Izak – she had memorized his name, and how could she not remember this beautiful name, which settled ever deeper into her heart, maybe into her soul, as it was the custom here to say – Izak, then, she could not see, neither him nor his violin, for the boy was playing in the summer house. But still, she was certain that nobody else could play so beautifully.

She did not want or dare to disturb this magnificent moment.

She did not know, in fact, how long she stood there listening, without moving a muscle. It was like being in the most beautiful coffee house in the world, the kind they don't have even in Paris perhaps, she later thought, as she lay in her bed recalling the events of the day.

And there was this, too: Izak, she felt, had been playing for her alone, maybe for the both of them, although this was something she did not dare to imagine.

Whether that was true or not, she knew that something beautiful had happened, something that could neither be repeated nor forgotten.

Her father's message, that the suit was ready to be fitted, she rattled off quickly to Mr Schwartz, right in the doorway to the shop, and then like a child ran home.

Her parents were waiting for her by the door, her father already in his coat, about to go looking for her. They knew that the German army had marched into town, and that the soldiers had right away started checking identification papers and making arrests in coffee houses and shops and in the streets. A neighbour had told them that the Germans had already shut down two stores with Jewish owners, without explanation, of course. Her parents, then, had plenty of reason to be worried, frightened and even angry with her.

So the family of Géza the tailor spent the entire afternoon sitting in the little front room. Her father could not calm his nerves: this was, perhaps, the first time he had been unable to sit quietly at his sewing machine and concentrate on his work. Every so often he would get up and start rummaging through his boxes, as if searching for something, and then sit down again without an answer. He knew very well that something terrible was being planned for the town, but he didn't know what it was or how it would be done.

Her mother stood by the stove polishing the silverware, over and over, as if she was trying to wipe away all the years and every morsel of food they had lifted to their mouths.

Edina, however, was filled with different thoughts, cheerful and playful. She was again happily spooling lengths of yarn, with an almost exaggerated enthusiasm.

'You'll run out of it by evening,' Edina's father said, almost calm now, as if the girl was proof that there was still hope in the world.

'You know, I heard him playing. It was so beautiful. You'd like it, too,' Edina said, more to herself than to her parents.

'Who?' they both asked at once.

'Why, Izak.' Edina blushed; she was almost embarrassed that she had to explain this. 'You know, the boy who's coming here tonight with his father, to be fitted.'

'Oh, is that why you were out so long? Well, at least you got to hear the concert. Otherwise you wouldn't have had the chance.'

'Why shouldn't we go to the coffee house? We never go to concerts!' Edina said firmly.

'Can't you see there's a war going on? And anyway, we haven't been invited,' her father said. 'Coffee houses and concerts are for upper-class folks, not tailors.'

'But even so…' Edina persisted, wanting to continue the debate.

'Quiet now. You're too young to understand. But I hope you will one day.'

As we said, dreams always come true.

Or maybe this can happen only once in our lives, like a great love, without us knowing either the time or the place.

Hope alone remains.

Edina may have understood this, although there was still much that she did not know.

Evening had settled in the window blinds. In the dark, clear sky, the stars were shining as always. It was as if there was no sadness in the world.

The soldiers, who had been stomping around town all day issuing random threats, were now lying low in the Sóbota school building.

Her father had pressed the suit one more time, as if he wanted to prove beyond doubt that he was truly a master tailor. From the bedroom came the sound of pages turning in a thick book. Edina, meanwhile, waited patiently to hear that jingling sound again.

It must be getting late; she could no longer count the chimes in the Lutheran church. Was that nine or ten? she wondered.

Then there really was somebody at the door. It had to be Izak and his father, she thought. But now there was no tiny jingle; maybe the angels had stayed behind, somewhere along the way. She could sense at once the anxiety, the unconcealed fear, in the hand that tapped briefly at the door.

'We couldn't leave home until after dark,' Mr Schwartz said in a whisper, as if someone had been following them. 'The streets are full of Hitler's watchmen. They've been going from house to house, but only to our houses. They're counting us and making a list of the Jews – I don't know why. People are saying we might be moved somewhere, taken out of town. I don't know what they want with us.'

'Come inside. No one will look for you here,' her father said, trying to calm his guest. 'Now let's try on that suit.'

'Look, Mr Šiftar, look at what they've ordered us to do. All Jews are required to wear a yellow Star of David on our clothes. They say it will make it easier for them to tell us apart. But what does that mean? Why do they have to tell us apart? We're no different from anyone else. Mrs Hirschl recently had a visit from Vienna. She says that her relatives there have to wear these stars all the time. I don't know what's going to happen to us.'

Edina could barely hide her tears. She again felt that fear, which in the course of the day had somehow melted away in the music, but now she could taste the poison and pain beneath her tongue.

Izak stepped behind the stove and changed into the new suit, re-sewn from his father's old one; then he stood beneath the oil lamp. She saw how his shoulders drooped, how his face was pale, without any glow. Maybe – the thought occurred to her – the wind had carried off all his music, as if Izak had given it away that morning, to everyone.

And now he could play only the silence.

'Mr Šiftar, you will need to sew this on, too. If a Jew does not have the Star of David sewn in a prominent place on his clothes, the punishment is prison.'

'Don't worry, Mr Schwartz, it will all be fine. Nothing should happen to honest people. I'll make sure this star looks beautiful on the suit.'

'One other thing,' the shopkeeper said, a little more cheerfully. 'My son, Izak, would like to invite you all to his concert at the coffee house. It's only right you be there; we are, after all, in your debt.'

At that moment something brightened in the room. Maybe the stars came out in the sky, or maybe it was only in their hearts.

They looked at each other and smiled, in a way that no one else would notice.

3

It wasn't often that the girl stayed at home alone on a Sunday. She had told her parents she wasn't feeling well, that she didn't want to go out in the rain, but really she just didn't feel like going to church. Her mother tried to change her mind – it wasn't right to leave her on her own, she said – but her father, surprisingly, took his daughter's side and was firm about it, despite his fears and doubts, as if for the first time in his life he felt able to stand up to anything. Of course, he couldn't explain this to himself, let alone to his wife, who kept asking him questions, all the way to the front gate of the church. It was troubling him even later, when the choir was singing – they were completely off-key that Sunday, which the organist must have noticed as well, because in the middle of playing he simply gave up and started singing with the congregation. For a moment the echo of the organ pipes continued to float above the nave, like that invisible eye which watches over everyone. Then, between the arches of the ceiling, beneath the choir loft and over the heads of the congregation, who were gazing at the image of the king with the crown of thorns, only voices remained, a tuneless singing, just one great sadness, lament and pain.

Géza the tailor felt for his wife's hand – she was singing softly, as if merely breathing out loud – and held it tightly. They both sensed there was a question here, one they would never, perhaps, be able to ask themselves, but whatever it might be, now, for a moment at least, they did not doubt that somewhere there was an answer, even if it were to remain a secret for all eternity. The one they were gazing at had perhaps not been crowned in vain.

The girl at home was looking out of a cross-framed window. As she had promised, she was staying in bed, although she did not really want to. She felt her heart – she heard it – beating inside her. It was pulling her outside somewhere; she needed to go out, to collect her thoughts, which were always eluding her. But she didn't have the strength to get up, and anyway, where could she go when the town was filled with those hateful soldiers? Mostly she wanted to hide, to bury herself beneath the covers, until these long, difficult days were over. Maybe she should have gone with her parents to church, should have been with other people, so that within those cold walls, listening to the singing and the words, she could soothe the fever racing through her. Of course, that was not really what she wanted either, and in fact there was an entirely different sort of music in her thoughts. Again she counted on her fingers how many days were left before the concert at the coffee house.

'Monday,' she began softly, and looked at the sky hanging over the town, pressing on it with an invisible finger – 'Tuesday' – the clouds, too, seemed to have tired themselves out and were slowly falling towards the silent earth, still bare and cold – 'Wednesday' – which even the birds had abandoned, as if fleeing from that eye. She saw it floating in the window, somewhere high above the wooden cross of the frame, saw it slowly opening.

Edina would often amuse herself by watching the clouds. She liked grazing the sheep, counting the teddy-bears and blinking at the sun. She marvelled at the mountains, which rose above the plain out of the dark, late-afternoon mists, radiant with red sun, especially since she had never seen any real mountains. But now it was all different. Of course, she was no longer afraid of the black storm clouds, and she understood, too, about thunder and lightning, but now, when she looked at that eye, which had acquired a fully defined shape, as if she had seen it somewhere before, she began to feel anxious. It was drawing her in, beckoning to her. The eye was watching her with a clarity that seemed more and more beautiful to her, perfect and exciting, like Izak's music the other day in the garden – yes, the feeling that now came over her she could compare only to music, and, at the same time, the nearer she came to that shape, as if she was floating, swimming, through the cross in the window, she felt she was losing herself, the music sinking into silence, the words blending into a monotone, in which there was one great sadness, but not death; elation, but not shouting. Maybe love, but she was unable to say this.

After the service, as people were standing up and the church was filled with whispers mingled with the scrape of the wooden pews on the floor, the clatter of footsteps and the smell of burnt-out candles, the tailor was still clasping his wife's hand. They remained seated, gazing into space, as if the words of Scripture were still echoing inside them: *They parted my raiment among them, and for my vesture they did cast lots.*

The men had already put on their hats, while the children could barely keep from running to the door and out into the garden in front of the church, where they would usually chase each other and play hide-and-seek until their overly worried parents found them – 'It's not right to play such loud games here,' the parents would say – but even so … The women, with bowed heads, humbly and seemingly lost in thought, as if they were still listening to a hymn that was fading away, were poking through their tiny purses, looking for a handkerchief or a small coin for a candle or special church service or, in particular, a new embroidered altar cloth. No one, surprisingly, was thinking of the war, the dead, the wounded or the missing, as if all of that was still somewhere far away, in a different world, or maybe no one had the courage to think of what was awaiting them, what they would no longer be able to hide from, not here any more. Or maybe, the words of Scripture were still echoing in them, too: *My kingdom is not of this world: if my kingdom were of this world, then would my servants fight that I not be delivered to the Jews: but now is my kingdom not from hence.*

A queue of humanity, big and little, proud and humble, was gathering in front of the door, which remained shut. At first, nobody was complaining or raising their voice or even looking up from the floor, as if they were the very embodiment of waiting, patience and humility. They just kept moving forward.

Before long they were rocking on their heels or walking in place, their backs to the enormous gold-adorned painting from which the one was watching whom they once had crowned and then forsaken.

'Open the door! Open it! So we can leave!' someone said after a while. His voice would surely have been lost in the crowd, among the bodies still pressing towards the exit, if someone at the end of the queue had not then shouted the same thing.

The tailor and his wife were still in the pew. They were the last ones sitting.

Now, when they heard the excited voices and the grumbling, which, clearly, was spreading rapidly from person to person and filling the space like a flood, the husband and wife exchanged glances. Of course, they did not immediately understand what was happening, for the silence was still inside them.

'*I am the door,*' a child's voice was then heard to say; he had jammed the door as a prank. The church overflowed with simple-hearted laughter, as if no one could understand.

'*Then from that day forth they took counsel together to put him to death.*' So was it written, and whispered, even after these silent, good people, who still knew how to talk about souls, had poured through the door and run like water down the steps. 'But still,' someone perhaps was thinking, 'was that ever truly forgiven?'

Now as they walked out, husband and wife, still holding hands, into the light of day, the last ones, with only emptiness behind them, they stood for a moment at the top of the steps, as they had done that first time together, in the same black suit and dress, he wearing a hat, she a veil.

That, too, had been a foggy April day, in 1931 – thirteen years ago. They had been laughing, although they had been almost alone, just as they were now. They had been young and expecting a child, who was already kicking in her mother's belly. The husband had picked up his wife and carried her down the steps. Then they walked bravely into the fog, but what happened later they had almost forgotten.

The same sort of fog – impenetrable and slow, swallowing up everything – was waiting for them at the door of the church, although now it was different, they felt. The outlines and shadows moving and disappearing in the distance, and in particular the indecipherable sounds, seemed to contain something menacing and mysterious, like a premonition. From where they stood, and maybe from anywhere, nothing was visible, let alone understandable.

From the street that led directly to the park and then, down a tree-lined promenade, to Sóbota Castle came the sound of stomping, of marching feet pounding and flattening the earth. Everything else was wrapped in a white, milky mirage, hidden even from that eye which still hovered above the *varaš*.

The tailor and his wife were walking towards the street when, by the church's front gate, they ran into two other couples, who were standing together and chatting. It was customary after the service for people to have a glass of wine or cup of coffee together at one of the coffee houses near the Lutheran church, most often, in fact, at the Dobray. Today, however, the Šiftars tried to excuse themselves, saying they were anxious to get home – indeed, they just wanted to have a mug of beer by themselves at Sočič's coffee house before hurrying home, where Edina would be expecting them; also, the tailor hoped to press the Schwartz boy's suit one more time before dinner, even though it was Sunday. He planned to deliver the order to the customer's home later that afternoon, as promised, and there, of course, he would make sure it was a proper fit.

But what could they do when Mrs Barbarič, and not just her but also Mrs Karas – and especially Mr Karas, who was always ready for a drink – would not let them leave? The Šiftars very rarely socialized with these couples, but they were the only people they met now. The fog that Sunday was truly doing its worst.

'The pastor spoke very well today, don't you think? And did you see his wife, and the fur she was wearing?' Mrs Barbarič began, as usual making the kind of remarks from which nobody was safe – especially now that her husband, who worked at the town hall, had recently received a promotion.

'Of course I saw her; how could one not? The poor thing was so cold she kept stroking her coat the whole time, even during the Apostles' Creed,' Mrs Karas merely added. 'Well, now at least your man can take you to Berger's, to pick out something warm and furry. I'm sure that Jew will have something in his shop to suit you.'

'Barbarič, did you hear what Mariška said?' Mrs Barbarič turned to her husband, and then to the other women she said: 'You see how it is with us – I'm of no value at all. Nobody listens to me in our house; it's like I don't exist.'

'Oh, surely not. Now that your husband's at the land registry, he will certainly take you shopping.'

'By the time that happens, all the Jewish shops will be closed, and he'll again be in luck!' she added with a big laugh.

'Well, at least there will finally be some order in Sóbota, like there is everywhere else,' Mr Barbarič, the new recorder at the land registry, said in a raised voice. 'The Germans know what they're doing. Not that I have anything against the Hungarians, mind you, but they haven't been able to bring those Jewish usurers to order. At the town hall, everyone says the town should be a town. A person can't just open some business in Sóbota and charge whatever they want. Those days are over. You'll see.'

'Just the other day our director, Mr Benko, was saying that we should leave the Jews in peace. Even though we do a fair amount of business with German meat dealers, the director says that the Germans' policies aren't completely right. That we should negotiate with them. The Jews, he says, are powerful and we need their connections and their shops. Who else are we going to sell wholesale to, if not to them?' This was Mr Karas speaking; he was a travelling salesman at the Benko meat factory.

'That's all politics, grand politics. But now we have the chance to show what we're made of! At the town hall, we're going to do things our way!'

Géza the tailor and his wife, walking arm in arm, were mostly silent, as if they had nothing to say, nothing to add to this peculiar small talk, which, in fact, may have been about only the fog. With every step, they were more and more convinced that they really should find some way to excuse themselves, to extricate themselves from such company, before they even reached the coffee house and ended up sitting too long over a glass of wine, as was very likely to happen.

'Will you be going to the concert on Wednesday?' the tailor's wife asked, for no other reason than to change the subject.

'What concert?' the others, surprised, asked in unison.

'At the Dobray. The Schwartz boy is giving his first concert! Géza even made a suit for him. It's sure to be wonderful. We've all been invited; Edina is so looking forward to it. As we are, too. It's been a long time since we went to a concert; you know, I can't remember the last time we did.'

For a moment, there was only silence among them. Maybe they were all thinking, or ignoring the question, or maybe it was just embarrassment, a misunderstanding, some inexplicable awkwardness, but whatever it was, the silence was more eloquent than words. They looked into the distance, at the empty street, at the *varaš*, which was hidden in fog.

The coffee house at the Hotel Dobray was filled with people treating themselves to a glass of good wine after church: the men were ordering a strong Lendava and mixing it with mineral water, while their wives and other ladies were enjoying a sweet Traminer from Radgona. Those who had arrived earlier, who had been sitting here all morning over coffee and the obligatory brandy, who had skipped divine services with little sense of guilt and preferred instead to discuss the latest news or read the German illustrated magazines, were already waiting for the goulash the waiters would soon be offering. When the tailor and his wife saw that the coffee house was packed, without a free table in sight, let alone any of the low tables by the tall windows, which is where they most enjoyed sitting at this hour of the day, they both thought for a moment and looked at each other, as if to say, now we could easily take our leave of these tiresome people and slip off somewhere on our own. They were no longer in the mood for a beer, let alone some overblown, empty conversation, nor were they particularly well versed in society politics, which was also why they did not come here very often. For while the Dobray was known primarily as a meeting place for the Sóbota elite, here, on Sundays, you could also find students and teachers, shopkeepers, journalists, civil servants and even workers from the rapidly growing local industries – butchers from Benko's, tailors from Cvetič's, carpenters from Hartner's sawmill – in short, everyone who, with their voices, complaints, silence and merriment contributed something to what for many was that incomprehensible coffee-house ambience.

Perhaps these people, the souls of these enthusiastic people, who, again and again, launched endless debates, played cards or demolished each other on black and white squares, could best be compared to fishermen, or travellers at deserted stations, or even poets, for they all had the feeling that they were waiting for something big, for inspiration, which, however, never comes back a second time.

But every so often someone would let something slip, long after night fell and when the gypsies were already playing from table to table, and people's heads were again empty and silent, as if they were slowly being occupied, being filled, by tender whispers. Then it might just occur to the ones who had been here a long time that somewhere a secret still lingered.

The three couples were waiting in the doorway, shifting from foot to foot as they tried to keep clear of the skilful waiters who were carrying large trays from the bar through the corridor to the salon, trying, more or less, to hold them high over their heads.

Šiftar was already extending his hand to the ladies – to Mariška Karas first and then Trezika Barbarič – when they were intercepted in the corridor by the hotelier and maître d' of the Dobray, Laci, who told them in amazement: 'I can't explain it! We're pouring drinks like there's no tomorrow! Dear ladies, gentlemen, please, come with me. I'll squeeze you in somewhere. I tell you, and please don't take this the wrong way, it might be Sunday, but it's a madhouse today.'

They were given seats in the corner by the last window, at a table that had been reserved for the musicians. Barbarič ordered wine and Petanjci mineral water for everyone – without asking the other two men or even glancing at the women.

'You see, everything is possible, you just need to find the right person,' he said pompously, as he laid his big wallet in the middle of the table, as if to say, drinks are on me today. 'You have to know how to handle people, especially waiters. That's what I always tell my Trezika – isn't that right, dear?'

'I was just about to say how things have really changed now that our good husband and father has been made a department head. And I'm not just talking about money, but attitudes, too. You see how everyone respects him. You know, I've been praying a long time for his success. The first time I saw him, I knew he'd be something big one day!'

Mrs Šiftar, who was sitting next to the window, looked outside. The fog, although still in the street, was slowly dissolving, thinning out in the sun, which was shining somewhere high overhead. The wine, too, which she wasn't used to, had warmed her cheeks, and her pallor had shyly melted into a gentle smile. Géza could detect a sparkle in her eyes.

Across the street, opposite the Hotel Dobray, Mr Ascher and his son were tidying the window display in the family's shop. The younger man was dusting and arranging the merchandise, while the father, with his pipe in his hand, kept checking the street, pacing back and forth, as if he was waiting for somebody.

'Oh, dear me! With that Benko, my husband has little chance of a promotion! He's still being sent into the field – whole days he's on his bicycle, riding around this unhappy land of ours. The only business he does is with farmers and Jews. I tell him sometimes: he needs to stand up for himself more. But the pay isn't bad.

Somewhere else it would be even harder to make ends meet. But all the same, you can see how thin he's become, just skin and bones – and at a butchery, too!' she concluded, and looked around the coffee house as if trying to examine the faces floating in the blue tobacco smoke. Then, her eyes seething with that distinctive look of spiteful envy, she leaned across the table and hissed: 'Just look at Benko over there, look at how big he is – like he's about to burst! Just like one of those pigs of his!'

'Laci, we'll have another round – the ladies are thirsty!' Karas, who placed the order, was obviously smarting, and not for the first time; he felt a burning inside that his Mariška would never be able to quench.

Géza remained silent, checking his pocket watch after every glass (which he had stopped counting). Every so often he would show a courteous smile, as if he was following the conversation, or give his wife a wink. By now they both realized they would not be getting out of here any time soon.

'The next round's on us,' Géza said, as Laci placed a chilled litre of wine and a bottle of mineral water on the table, and then, although he knew it wasn't polite, he retreated into his thoughts again. He began listening to the conversation at the table behind him.

'I knew those Hungarian court councillors would flee at the first whiff of smoke over Budapest. Now that an English bomb has dropped from the sky, that admiral without a sea, Nikolaus von Horthy, is pulling back his invisible fleet. My only question is, where will they go into hiding – Lake Balaton, perchance?'

'I'm more concerned about what's going to happen to us. What action are we Slovenes going to take? We're trapped here, in this unhappy land of ours. Clearly, we can't rely on the establishment any more. Hartner is already changing his tune. I hear he's parted ways with the Hungarian Life Party, where he's been trying for so long to pass us Slovenes off as Hungarians. And now that they're falling apart, he'd like to make a present of us to the Germans. I tell you, it's our last chance, the clock is ticking. We're going to have to perform, to start playing on the big stage.'

'I'm afraid – I'm seriously afraid – that it may be too late for us. Today, in fact, might be the last time we have drinks at our beloved Dobray. The Germans are different. You see them: they haven't even settled in and already they're baring their teeth. If anyone can bring us to our knees, it's them.'

'But what about the Russians?' a third person at the table chimed in, but before Géza could catch his point, he was startled by his wife's voice.

'Look! Look what they're doing to them!' she said, appalled. She was still gazing out of the window. Géza glanced at his wife's pale face. She was trembling all over in shock and alarm. Now they were both on their feet – he, because he wanted to move closer to her, to try to calm her down; she, because she could no longer remain seated. Amazingly, nobody else had moved, as if they had neither heard nor seen anything.

Across the street, opposite the Hotel Dobray, a military motor-cycle with a sidecar had stopped in front of Ascher's shop, where the shopkeeper and his son were still standing. A German officer in a long black coat with a swastika on the sleeve climbed out of the sidecar. He quickly went over to the two men in front of the shop, who stood there as if rooted to the ground. With a short baton, which he was turning in his hands, the officer shoved the men away from the wall. Now the driver, too, got off the motorcycle, which remained running, took a small canister that had been hanging from the handlebars, and walked over to the officer.

'The SS,' said someone in the coffee house who had recognized the two military men.

Géza now had his arm around his wife. They watched as the first man used his baton to make an invisible star on the chest of the elder Ascher, who was leaning against the wall of his shop. Meanwhile, the other one splashed some black paint on the just-washed shop window and sloppily, with a wide brush, shaped the glob into a big Star of David.

'Outrageous, outrageous!' This was the only voice heard in the coffee house, which, at the scene across the street, had suddenly fallen silent. 'Goddamn upper classes! You don't care about anything but your own arses!' cried a young man, a student named Gašparič, who was emboldened by the wine and, especially, by *The Young Prekmurian*, a now-defunct journal in which the region's future intelligentsia, educated in Maribor and Ljubljana, had contributed articles and bravely made themselves heard, and which had been avidly read by boys and young men. 'Can't you wretched fools see that this is what we Slovenes have to look forward to! The world is falling apart, and all you do is wait for something to happen.'

He was shouting, even though he knew the Gestapo had their eye on him and that by now their informants were even in the coffee house.

The tailor and his wife stood for a moment on the doorstep of the Hotel Dobray. The fog, in which the *varaš* had bashfully been hiding just a short while earlier, had now dissolved in the midday sun. The streets around Main Square were empty, and in front of Ascher's shop, too, everything was quiet. The black star on the shop window had dried quickly, and no one would now be able to wash it off. It would remain for a long time, shining there, a dark sign it might never be possible to remove.

Géza draped his coat over his wife's frail body, and from the corners of their eyes they looked at the poster on the door, which was advertising the violin concert on Wednesday. He felt his wife shudder, as if she was naked in the fog.

Before they stepped into the street, the husband dropped some coins onto the palm of a gypsy woman, who seemed to have appeared out of nowhere. But Sunday, the couple knew, was not a day for fortune telling.

That was when a bit of music slipped out of the hotel. It was the same sad melody, the kind only weary fiddlers were able to play, who bent the dusty roads beneath their knobbly fingers and conjured up the trackless expanses that led, as nothing else could, to the other side. This, these fiddlers knew, was music that made every throat dry and every heart softer. Again, for a moment, they were on the trail of the lost soul, and close was the thought that somewhere the secret still existed – the thing that should never have been lost.

Perhaps, there was again something great inside them, or maybe it was only the silence.

4

Long into the night, the girl was again spooling the black lengths of yarn and listening as her mother read out loud. The words about good people and mysterious places wove themselves into the marvellous garment that was emerging beneath her father's diligent hands. She was spooling the black lengths even after the yarn had run out and she was merely dreaming.

The whir of the sewing machine gives way to the thrum of a big bicycle riding on water. It's as though she is part of the eye that hovers high in the air. She sees a boy riding a man's bicycle down a silent and slow Pannonian river, and the only thing left on the surface is a black trail, sharp as a violin string, and it is resonating. She knows he cannot see her, yet he senses that she is with him. He is going away, sinking into the evening, disappearing around the bend. Soon all that remains is the resonating sound, a voice above the dark river, which never truly fades.

On Wednesday, April 26, 1944, not long before five o'clock, a small group of people were gathered on the steps of the Hotel Dobray. Not many still remember that it was cold and bleak that day. The grey that covered the sky was blurring the shadows – the town seemed wrapped in silence, sunk in a long, afternoon doze.

'A Siberian wind is blowing,' the men whispered as they paced back and forth around their wives, who despite the cold were trying to preserve their dignity. The women were patiently waiting to at last be asked in, out of the weather. They remained silent, as if expanses were opening within them and they alone could hear the voice that was carried on the wind. Something must have been pulling them far away, to where that cold spirit was coming from, which had found its way beneath the ladies' light coats. They felt their souls turning to ice, but they had no way of showing this. Or maybe it was just a feeling, an uneasiness at the sight of this handful of frightened people, who after the events of recent days had nothing left but hope – so everyone was now trying to think only about the concert, the music of the young Izak Schwartz, who was about to give his debut performance.

'They're going to take everything away from us. They'll destroy everything we have,' Mr Hoyer was saying. 'You see how they've shut down our shops already. What are we going to live on?'

'Let them do what they want, so long as they leave us and our children in peace. I hear they're starting to lock people up, and sending them away, too. But I don't believe the Hungarians will let them do that to us – because what did we ever do to them? We have always behaved properly towards them.'

This was Mr Blau, whose shop the Germans had sealed the day before; and they had seized all his merchandise, too: he was holding out hope that his complaint in Budapest would succeed. He was well connected there to lawyers and Horthy officials, people he saw regularly on his business trips to the capital and richly supplied with the finest wines and choice trinkets for their ladies, as he put it.

'It will not end well. Don't you listen to the radio? Those Hungarian dreams are over. The West won't be easy on them any more now that they're cosying up to the Reich. The Hungarians don't need us now; they'll sell us out to Hitler, and cheap, too, just so their aristocrats can go on dancing.'

'I know that, I know everything, only the Hungarians are also afraid of the Russians, who in any case, people are saying, will take away everything we have.'

'We need to be united. Our elders should do something for us. In Budapest, people have left everything to be handled by the Jewish Council, which is organizing their documents for them. If there's no life left for us here, we have to be ready to leave.'

'But where's a poor Jew to go?' The young Hirschl was now speaking, too loudly, so the entire group woke up at once, as if some forgotten alarm clock had gone off. 'Are we just going to start walking, wandering around like that lost man Rabbi Roth tells us about?'

'Now is not the time for fairy tales. We've already packed our bags – we're leaving on the first train, to somewhere,' Mr Ascher said with conviction. He had made all the preparations on Sunday, after the SS men defaced his window.

'But where? Where can we go, I ask you? Can't you see? The carriages are all full. There is no place, no peace any more, for Jews in this unhappy land, and Jerusalem, which we've been promised, is far away. Can't you read what they write? Plenty are willing, but few are chosen!'

'Oh, my dear Judit, do you have any idea what young Schwartz will be playing today? The poster doesn't say.' The women were chatting as if they did not want to hear or know what the men were discussing, since it was no longer just about music.

'I heard someone say that the young man plays Brahms's *Hungarian Dances* splendidly, and there will also be a band – a gypsy band, of course. It should be something to hear!'

The Šiftars arrived just a few minutes before five. A small group of well-dressed men and women were clustered by the door of the Hotel Dobray, which was still closed. In the tall windows, which looked on the garden beneath the chestnuts, the heavy red curtains were half drawn. There was a faint light behind them; the tinted chandeliers, which were usually turned on throughout the day, so it was always pleasantly bright inside the coffee house, remained dark.

The people shuffling their feet near the entrance were by now thoroughly chilled by the wind. The men standing on the highest step had taken off their hats; they had their noses pressed to the glass door and were peering into the empty corridor. This was where the hotelier, Laci, would usually be welcoming guests, but now there was no one in sight.

'In the big salon, where they're supposed to play, it's still dark!' The news spread quickly through the group.

'That can't be true!'

'What can they be up to? It's those Hitlerites who've done this. So what are we going to do now?'

'Has anyone seen Mr Schwartz? We need to speak to him!'

'Well, someone should at least tell us something. They can't just shut down the Dobray like this.'

Edina was standing between her mother and her father. They had placed themselves next to the last chestnut tree in front of the hotel, as if they felt they somehow did not belong. Although her family had never been unsociable, Edina was feeling rather awkward, strange, even that it was pointless for them to be there. Of course she couldn't understand; there were countless thoughts inside her, now smouldering, now burning again. She felt ashamed, her cheeks were glowing, she wasn't used to polite society, that coffee-house ambience, well-chosen words and covert insinuations; but at the same time her heart was pounding with an anticipation so strong she could barely contain it: she would see young Izak, hear his heavenly music again – it was all making her feel like she could fly. But there was also anger here, the first unhealed wound, which she simply could not forget, and certainly not forgive – yes, who could imagine it, who could seriously put up with it? she had thought more than once; in any case, there was a mischievous smile on her face, because when she and her father had gone to their house on Sunday evening to deliver the suit, he was nowhere in sight. She knew it wasn't really proper for her to accompany her father on business visits to strangers' homes, but she had gone anyway, if only because, despite everything, her father understood. And then the boy had refused to show himself. Mr Schwartz had politely and sympathetically apologized for his son in a few simple words: 'Izak is very sorry, but he needs to practise, you know.' For her, it was as if he had plunged her in icy water, left her standing outside the door, killed her – yes, even that, she thought, although she could not imagine what *that* might look like. But she felt it. She had heard him playing upstairs; she knew he was standing in the middle of the drawing room, somewhere directly above her. It was one of the most beautiful things she had ever experienced, and although he was playing the same composition he had played in the summer house, it was entirely different. Now in his playing there was something heavy, painful, deep and slow, as if it had no beginning and no end. It revealed itself to her, and it hurt, but it was not for tears; it was sublimely beautiful, but it was not for the eye. An angel, she thought, never dies. This music cannot be from here; I just wanted to see him one more time, she lied, slightly, to herself. Oh, if only I could see him – this had been racing through her ever since, up until this very moment, as she stood between her mother and her father and for the first time in her life had nobody to tell. She was only waiting, just as she was.

At exactly five o'clock – the bells were chiming from both Sóbota belfries – a motorcycle with a sidecar appeared in the street in front of the Hotel Dobray. The rumble and putter that pierced the ears of the concert-goers held their attention for only a short time – by now they were accustomed to such scenes. They were sure this was yet another demonstration of the power and hollow self-importance of the army, which had not yet fully settled into this little nest, this *varaš*, which was still trying to get used to the new uniforms.

The motorcycle, however, neither stopped nor rumbled down the dusty street. A uniformed man, who had been immersed up to his neck in the sidecar, now scrambled to his feet and pointed at the hotel with his arm. The driver turned and drove straight at the people, who instinctively pressed themselves against the door.

The Šiftars, too, were speechless. A void now opened between them and the people near the door, who suddenly seemed further away than they had ever imagined. That was when Edina realized they were all marked; only now did she understand why they had to wear those star-shaped patches.

People who just a few days earlier had been neighbours, shop-keepers, acquaintances, friends or even strangers, were now simply Jews, all without distinction, without name, face or language. And in this entire crowd of people who were more or less the same, she thought of only one: Izak – the name stuck in her throat.

'Let's go,' she said, grabbing her mother's and father's hands. 'Let's go inside,' she was saying as she pulled her parents forward. But she could feel that they were rooted to the ground, tied to the tree.

'Wait,' her father said softly.

She let go of their hands and started to run. Before her father could reach her, she was already in the thick of the crowd.

The figure in the elegant black uniform – he seemed to be dressed for the concert – climbed gingerly out of the low sidecar, just a step from the door of the Hotel Dobray. The wary group of Jews, now squeezing together even more, made way for the officer, who slowly, rather haughtily, and with an air of indifference, proceeded to the door in high, well-polished boots. It was as if everyone had long been rehearsing this scene, as if the entire thing was merely being repeated – and maybe it truly was just theatre, something unreal, only nobody at the time could say who was the audience and who was acting.

Without looking around or stopping at the door, the apparition in the black uniform opened it with confidence. At this gesture, which concealed some mysterious power, only sighs could be heard from the crowd, as if they felt relieved; at the same time, one sensed in their sighing a certain inexplicable respect, a devotion, as if something had again revealed itself to them. They stood as if spellbound – the door at which they had been waiting helplessly for so long was now wide open; they need only enter. The figure, meanwhile, had vanished, and a man in a black uniform, with short, painful steps, was climbing the stairs to the first floor.

The girl, trapped and pressed between bodies, was suffocating, drowning in murky water; all around her she felt sharp elbows, shoulders and knees, which were trying to keep the people upright; in the waves of sighing, coughing and murmuring, she caught the sound of her name, as if for an instant she had floated to the surface, before that human vortex dragged her under again. Father, Mama – this was running through her consciousness – they're searching for me. She was on her knees now, looking up, towards the light hovering in the gaps between the edges of the black hats, the terrified, surprised faces and the clenched arms, while looming above them, like a mighty underwater wall, with caves, cathedrals and concert halls, was the dark façade of the Hotel Dobray, and just before she fainted, somewhere high above everything, that same mighty eye appeared, which she had watched through her window at home. Then the pressure eased, the bodies separated, like water draining, and she was lying in front of the steps, in darkness, and she thought: this mighty eye, through which she was watching herself, would never again leave her.

5

It was not until a full year later that Edina learned what had happened that fateful night, on April 26, 1944, when Izak's debut concert was cancelled.

The Jews who had gathered in front of the Hotel Dobray never did enter the salon; the only people sitting there, in the front row, were two women: Linna, who had arrived in town that morning, and her real mother, Sugar Neni, who, however, never revealed that to her.

A few minutes after five o'clock, the Nazis loaded Izak's family onto a lorry, along with the concert-goers, and took them to the railway station, where they were packed onto a train. They were accompanied by the Dobray's coffee-house orchestra, who had never played so well.

That night they were taken by rail to Čakovec and from there, the very next morning, to Auschwitz, in Poland.

There, children were separated from their mothers, and husbands from their wives. Those who were able to work laboured for a time before dying under the brutal conditions.

The others they stripped of their clothes, confiscated all their belongings, shaved their heads and herded into enormous washrooms. Instead of water, they released lethal gas. After that, they just burned the corpses in crematoria, which operated like big factories.

All four hundred Prekmurian Jews were deported to Auschwitz and other camps in a single night. Only twenty-six returned after the war, including Franz Schwartz.

The Jewish community in Sóbota, which in the years before the war had been one of the largest in all of Yugoslavia, never recovered.

Nearly eradicated, impoverished and profoundly stigmatized, the Jews of Sóbota were no longer able to form a minyan, the quorum of ten adult male believers required for the ritual reading of the Sefer Torah in the synagogue, which therefore remained closed after the war.

When, after numerous break-ins and thefts, people had virtually destroyed the synagogue, the army turned the building into a stable for horses.

In 1954, the Sóbota authorities had the synagogue torn down. Not long afterwards, in its place, the first modern apartment block in Murska Sobota was erected; it was designed by the architect Feri Novak. Even today people call the building 'the Jewish block'.

Stalin's
Pipe Organ

1

That Friday crept along like a low-flowing river. But if the day already seemed long, the feeling that time had slowed down was now getting even stronger. Ever since the trumpets had grown quiet that had been leading unbroken columns of soldiers through these parts day and night, the plain was resonating again. It was a strange, indefinable sound that inhabited the soul. It was perhaps only silence, but it was the kind that settles deep inside a person, like a fistful of cold water. Such a person never again feels thirst or the need to waste unnecessary words on it. The ghastly music of Stalin's pipe organ was still echoing only in the ears of a very few. In them was preserved an image branded in golden ashes. It glowed with every inhalation, like tobacco in a pipe. Franz Schwartz had such eyes.

And this Friday, as he unfolded the newspaper in which his lunch was wrapped, he recalled for a moment the faith that had long ago died within him. He alone felt that terrible conscience, which beat him like a dead father with whom reconciliation was impossible. All the good he had was lying in front of him on this old counter. A lump of fresh curd cheese, bread, a few grains of sugar. Before starting on his dinner, he shook the ash out of his hot pipe, which he was always packing with too-dry tobacco, then went over to the tall shop window and cautiously closed the yellowed curtain. The soulless world, which had taken from him everything he loved, remained on the other side. Now it was even darker in the cramped boutique (in his thoughts he still used the old term to refer to this second-hand clothing shop). But nobody would disturb him as he went to the metal chest hidden at the back of the room, like the Holy of Holies in the Temple. He always had the key with him, tucked between the papers in his thick wallet, which he carried in the right back pocket of his trousers. Now he carefully pulled out the wallet and burrowed with his bony fingers among the papers and old photographs. Here were all his riches stored: dozens of papers – expired documents, crumpled scraps written over in a shopkeeper's hand and, of course, the faded photographs, which more and more rarely, and with great apprehension, he would draw out into the light.

For a brief moment his trembling fingers froze, as if he was debating whether to unfurl all this precious content yet again or leave the pain alone. The idea of simply throwing away or burning this whole great burden – he dare not think about it. Then his fingers felt the tiny key, which he pulled into his hand, and instantly the papers were again safely sealed away in his dark pocket. He deftly inserted the key in its slot and opened the rickety cash box. Despite the darkness, something glistened in his eyes. With pride and satisfaction, such as he rarely found now in the world, he treated himself to his last jar of honey.

On that long Friday, which possibly would never pass into Saturday, for the silent shop manager Franz Schwartz, former proprietor of a general store, this was sufficient.

The manager of a shop that sold second-hand garments for ladies and men – there was only a small sample of new clothes in the boutique, and even those were from wartime, collected from abandoned homes – was sitting on a stool, leaning his elbows on the counter. In front of him was an empty jar of honey, now filled with water. The last traces of the sweet sun were slowly dissolving in the cloudy liquid. Ordinarily, he would boil the sweetish solution and pour it over camomile or elderberry blossoms, but now he didn't even have those. He had not walked through meadows or woods in a long time. Or rather, the last time he had, he was fleeing death. He couldn't resist. He grabbed the jar – some of the thick, sticky liquid ran down his hand and dribbled on the creaky floorboards – and went to the door.

He stood on the threshold, looking out at the red mists of the late afternoon, stretched low above the silent houses. Fire grazed the rooftops and descended all the way down to the dust-caked windows, which then glowed with tired eyes. The houses seemed to be suffocating in smoke leaking from an old stove. He felt the anxiety and fear that gripped the people behind the thick blinds. But still there was nobody going up to their window now, maybe even opening it, to glimpse the beauty of the sky as it passed into night.

Sóbota will perish without witnesses. The Lord will walk alone down Main Street without hearing a word of praise, and will destroy what is meant for destruction – this was the warning a good angel delivered to Franz Schwartz.

The darkness, loneliness and despair in which people had immured themselves would not protect them from the judgement that was to fall upon the righteous. Long would they remember the evening when the one who was sent to them did what he had come to do. This image cannot be erased. It will burn for as long as people still call each other by name.

The shopkeeper's musings were cut short by the rumble and putter of a motorcycle slicing through the dust down Main Street. He hastily retreated into the shop. He knew that sound. There were not many motorcycles here, but this one had left a special impression on his hearing. There was something about its rhythm that everyone recognized even from a distance. It was like a clock striking thirteen. Franz Schwartz suspected that this impossible hour would be striking more and more often from now on, that it would soon drown out the bells in all the bell towers and that it would keep striking until every last soul was converted. What demon, he wondered, had created this monstrous mechanism, whose sound had captivated so many?

Now the shop manager – before the war, proprietor of a general store, Jew and respected merchant – picked up a cloth and slowly got down on his knees. He was wiping off the honey stains, which had already dried into the floor. He wiped them up meticulously, with wide strokes, as if every drop was precious. As he did this, he recalled the time when, still just an apprentice in his father's shop, he had broken a jar full of ground cinnamon; in fear, and wanting to hide the damage, he had brushed the fragrant powder into his cap. But he never could keep anything from his mother: as soon as he walked into the house, when she greeted him with a kiss on the forehead, the secret was out. For a long time his family would tease him about this around the dinner table, whenever they remembered his aromatic scalp.

Suddenly, there was that rumble again. It surprised him how extremely close it was. Before he could get up and peek out from behind the curtain, the light door of the shop swung open. The black motorcycle with the sidecar was more or less parked on his threshold. A yellowish beam of light shone from a narrow, shaded slit on the handlebar. The shopkeeper froze. Still on his knees, he stared into that light.

A creature in a long leather coat and soft helmet, which covered his watery head, stepped off the motorcycle. The eyes, hidden behind black motoring goggles, no one had yet seen. At least that is what those who had met him said. But there was one thing everyone could agree on: this creature could not be human.

Franz Schwartz, shopkeeper and manager, had of course heard people talking numerous times about the tough-as-nails field worker who had been sent here from the Ljubljana office of OZNA, the secret police, with special authorization and a single task: to liquidate the entire former bourgeoisie, as well as anyone still trying to act superior. The effect was total. After only a few days, the muted fear people carried within them, instilled by the just-ended war, had burst into flames. But they had no name for what was suffocating them. It was something intermixed with triumph, despair and envy. Mortal fear again acquired human form. Everyone was desperately trying to satisfy the massive appetite shown by the newborn freedom. But the only ones laughing were the drunks and those with a special gift, who in everything saw unbridled, proliferating madness.

This was all going through Franz Schwartz's mind at that moment, when he was still on his knees. But he was not afraid. He had been through much worse, at least that's what he thought, and now, rather naively, he was simply astonished by that freak of nature with the big hump, which made him seem more pitiful than frightening. Hunchback Miha – as everybody called him, although nobody was brave enough to look at his hump, or even his eyes, for that matter – was now standing in front of the boutique examining the modest window display. He paid no attention at all to Franz, as if human weakness and curiosity had, for just a moment, been reawakened within him – seeing this shop window, perhaps, reminded him of some never-fulfilled boyish desire. Surely, like anyone, he must have once wished for a new suit, or at least a hat, that would make him more attractive; maybe he had thought of asking some girl to the cinema and that splendid suit would certainly hide the hump; a sports jacket with gold buttons would dazzle many a girl, who would then see a young gentleman wearing it and not some cripple. But the thought of young gentlemen in handsome suits and soft hats, especially well-heeled young gentlemen, the kind all girls liked, brought him back to reality at once. That's not what I'm here for! he thought, cursing his weakness, and he was again on the campaign: the upper classes must be liquidated, now we are all equal – the memorized phrases echoed in his head. We fought too long to have our freedom fashioned by gold-buttoned gentlemen.

Hunchback Miha, specially authorized OZNA political agent and liquidator, soon collected himself. Orders must be obeyed unconditionally. Until the revolution is complete and freedom is purged of every person who mourns the old days, we must work. Work with guns, too, somebody whispered in his ear. The motor-cycle was still rumbling and puttering. But the agent from OZNA, it seemed, was not sure what to do.

He turned to the motorcycle and yelled, 'Give it here!' – and in fact, an arm then reached out of the sidecar. Until now, Franz had not been able to see his associate, who was lying drunk in the sidecar. The man could barely pull himself up and hand his boss the booze. He must have been unconscious: his eyes were rolled back into his head, his mouth was drooling and his body was completely limp, but still he obeyed unconditionally. Hunchback Miha took a long draught – Franz could hear him guzzling down air and the toxic spirits. The man in the sidecar was laughing. When the OZNA agent ran out of breath, his face entirely red, he lowered the glass and spat out a bloody gob of phlegm. 'Shut up!' he growled, and hurled the empty glass at his associate's head. 'You drive!' he ordered. The other man, without hesitating, tumbled out of the sidecar and onto the motorcycle, which, with childlike enthusiasm, he pulled away from the threshold.

Franz Schwartz dragged himself on his knees deeper into the shop. He was still not sure if the OZNA agents had seen him. He was now watching the enormous shadow on the other side of the shop-window curtain. He saw a sudden movement of the shadow's right arm, which flew into the air and then, as if chopping wood, swung down and struck the window glass. There was a bang and a jingling, like hundreds of crystal glasses colliding. But, to his amazement, the window pane remained intact.

'Jewish pigs!' the shadow roared like a wounded beast; it was the first time he had faced something that resisted him. He was used to shooting people between the eyes, to liquidations; without a twinge of conscience he had borne the pleading, the sobbing, the despair of the condemned, whom he himself had chosen – after all, he had verbal authorization from Ljubljana, from headquarters. But then something like this happens. 'Go! Go!' he howled in despair at his drunken associate, who, upon witnessing this miracle, had almost sobered up. Never before had he seen his colleague, which is to say his boss, so powerless and angry. Death aroused no compassion in Hunchback Miha, who did not even need to drink when they went into the field. But as for him, he didn't dare piss any more without a drink. He was convinced that one day he would piss out the blood of everyone they had killed. His only consolation was that he was merely the associate here: mostly, he just watched the motorcycle whenever Hunchback Miha, the chief OZNA agent, found himself delayed in conversation with one of those bourgeois pigs, Jews or idlers, who did not yet feel themselves free in their new motherland.

Still, more and more often, he heard a voice inside him saying there would be hell to pay. He was all in knots, and not even alcohol could loosen them any more. For a long time his father had beat him, when he was still just a child, but he hadn't felt it then; now, the old wounds had reopened and his entire body was in pain, even if there were no visible marks. The freedom that had arrived, he sensed, could not absolve sin – somewhere there would always be a voice begging: *Don't kill me!*

If he had not at that moment bolted off on the motorcycle, towards Court Street, that crazy Miha would undoubtedly have shot him in the face.

Franz Schwartz saw the barrel of the pistol protruding from behind the frame of the door. But the humped body remained veiled by the shop-window curtain.

Outside, darkness had finally fallen. It was Friday evening, and soon the candles would have to be lit on the well-laid tables and the oldest Jew could then calmly break off the first piece of the Sabbath bread. But all the windows in the town, which just a minute before had glowed with the light of late afternoon, remained black, as if the last spark of life had flickered out of the dying. The dust and especially the putter of the motorcycle, as it disappeared down Court Street, had subsided. There was only silence. It was dark, too, inside the second-hand clothes boutique. The shop manager was still on his knees, pressing to his lips a cloth that smelled of honey, to muffle his heavy breathing and calm his heart. He continued to gaze at the pistol, which was still hanging in the air.

2

Although the war, to all intents and purposes, had ended in Prekmurje in the first days of April 1945, more than a month before the guns fell silent in the rest of Slovenia and throughout Europe – Ljubljana, for example, was not liberated until May 9 – fatalities continued right up to April 11, mostly on the battlefront along the Mura River, where the retreating German army had again entrenched its positions. On the banks of the river and in the dead pools, lying alongside Yugoslav Partisans and Prekmurians, who experienced the full horror of battle only as the war was reaching its end, most of the dead were Red Army soldiers, who would later be buried in a common tomb in the Sóbota cemetery.

Despite their enormous losses – and their ultimate success in breaching the front line, owing to the soldiers' immense dedication and with the help of that mysterious weapon, the Katyusha rocket launcher, which people here called Stalin's pipe organ and which very likely decided the victory on the Mura – the Red Army never crossed the river.

Although the bloody fighting on the Mura continued, the new people's government in Prekmurje was set up swiftly, thanks primarily to the high degree of readiness of the Liberation Front committees, which throughout March had been working underground to prepare for the assumption of power. Thus, as early as April 4, a two-day meeting was convened in Murska Sobota, attended by most of the local Partisans and LF activists. They agreed that they needed first of all to take control of the post offices, municipal offices and shops in every locality in the region. Over the next few days encouraging messages were arriving at the headquarters of the Liberation Front for Prekmurje, saying that the assumption of power and seizure of private property were proceeding 'very normally, in a well-regulated manner, with no major anomalies'. The organs of the new power ascribed the credit for this achievement 'first and foremost to good organization and, especially, to the Prekmurians' respect and full support for the new government'.

The confiscated property, in particular the shops, workshops and factories, were handed over to the new people's government to manage and use as they saw fit. An official register of the population was introduced, to which were added the names of the returnees, the permanently displaced and the war dead. Franz Schwartz presented himself to the new municipal committee in Murska Sobota on April 3, 1945.

When he appeared for registration, the clerk, who was sitting behind a long table that had been set up for this purpose in the courtyard of the town hall, insisted – absolutely insisted, as she repeated more than once – that he use his Slovene name. She registered him as 'Franc ŠVARC – deportee, camp returnee' and, for his wife and son, ticked the box 'permanently missing'. He was obliged to declare all his private property, which was then carefully listed and nationalized.

As a former shopkeeper, he was allocated, 'in the capacity of his general work obligation', a small boutique, or rather, used clothing shop, on Main Street; this, in fact, was nothing more than a walled-off corridor, where he had to organize the space as best he could. And there was a shack in the courtyard where he could live.

New merchandise was impossible to come by, so he was given explicit orders to collect, as soon as possible, all clothes left behind in the abandoned and nationalized houses, most of which had belonged to Jews who never returned from the camps or to wealthy townspeople whose dwellings had recently been seized.

A few days later, confiscated military uniforms were also delivered to him – German, Hungarian and Russian – mostly from fallen or captured soldiers. There were, however, among the piles of filthy, torn and blood-stained clothes, also many civilian garments, which had belonged to men, women and children, to everyone the victorious Partisans had recently interned in improvised camps, one of the largest of which, surrounded by barbed wire, was set up on the plain, not far from Filovci.

The shopkeeper first tore the insignia off the uniforms, which he then cleaned and exchanged for food vouchers with workers, who later wore them while constructing and restoring buildings, roads and towns.

As for the civilian garments, which consisted mostly of Sunday clothes, black and grey overcoats and women's suits and dresses worn mainly by townspeople and wealthy farmers, Franz merely brushed them, emptied their pockets and hung them on the walls, one on top of the other. The best parts of a military uniform that had remained undamaged he displayed in the shop window along with a cap and boots – this appealed, in particular, to the many officers and directors who had risen to their high ranks and positions literally overnight.

By that Friday evening, when the shopkeeper Franz Schwartz was on his knees late into the night, gazing at the shadow in the display window, it was already generally known and being talked about throughout the town, where there were never any secrets, that some farmers had found a body near the road to Črnske Meje. At first the farmers were sure the man must have been shot by God only knows which of the armies that had passed through here in quick succession. Then they were sure he must have been part of the group of hostages that had been found shot to death deep in the Črnske Meje woods, only the hostages' hands had been tied and their eyes blindfolded, and they had all been barefoot, their boots and shoes taken by their executioners, who were anticipating a long road ahead.

The hostages had been brought to Črnske Meje from the Sóbota prison right after that cross-shooting at horses, when József Sárdy and his terrified army withdrew from the town. Sárdy had used the prisoners as a human shield because he was convinced that the town was already swarming with Russians, who in fact were still relatively far away. Once outside Sóbota, he ordered the prisoners to be shot, plain and simple.

Unlike the hostages, the dead man near the road was warmly dressed and well attired, and, most significantly, he was found far from the site of the mass killings.

But when they turned the body on its back, the farmers gasped. The man, who must have been lying in the mud for several days, was entirely without a face and, essentially, unrecognizable. His cheeks had been bashed in and scraped to the bone, and his teeth and jaws were so broken that his face was in two pieces. His eyes had fallen deep into the sockets, and soil was oozing out of the gaping hole where his mouth had been. They found no gunshot wound, a fact that seriously alarmed them. Who, they wondered, could have used such force, with their bare hands, against this young and healthy man?

Not far from the body they found an expensive fur collar and a pair of stylish shoes, the kind not many women here wore – this quickly elicited insinuations and rumours throughout the area. Somewhat further away, near the woods, they found a lady's coat to which the fur seemed to belong.

Since what first caught their eye had been a postal bicycle, they thought it best to bring the body and the other things they had found to the post office, where maybe someone would recognize the man – and to do this before it was all stolen by the crows, which were already flocking nearby.

They loaded everything into a big wheelbarrow, which they then pushed through the entire town to the post office, where a crowd of inquisitive onlookers had already started to form.

The farmers – who were still, unreasonably, claiming owner-ship of their find, including the valuable items – laid everything out carefully in front of the post office as if they were at a flea market. With pale faces or covert mockery, people leaned over to inspect the objects. The women, mostly horrified, were trying to force themselves to look at the mutilated body, in the hope that they might recognize the person, while the men were more concerned with guessing and speculating about the owner of those posh suede shoes and, especially, that fur. They couldn't make sense of it all, couldn't imagine what had happened.

Clearly, the long years of war and then the swift and sudden freedom, which came sooner here than anyone expected, had left their mark – people, it seemed, had grown accustomed to death and then, overnight, to the new regime, which promised them liberty and prosperity. For although blood was still flowing every-where, the passions that had been long suppressed in the town quickly burst into life. It was as though the lives of other people no longer had value; in this vacuum between war and peace, life and death, everyone was watching out only for their own arse, as people said.

And indeed, the crowd in front of the post office now exploded, burst into life. They became loud; some were drinking *palinka*, others were cadging tobacco, which miraculously had appeared again on the black market. Everyone was talking about that coat and those suede shoes, and also about tomorrow's rally, the first rally in honour of the liberation.

The crowd did not calm down until a gun was fired in the air by the new town secretary and member of the local presidium of the Liberation Front, Comrade Barbarič. He had been elevated to this high office purportedly because of his abilities: throughout the past month, he had shown himself to be an extremely loyal and reliable operative. His bureaucratic experience, too, had proved essential; having previously served as secretary of the land registry, he knew the weaknesses of the old government inside out.

Now, for the first time, he was standing in front of a crowd with a gun in his hand and he could barely hide the fact that he was cold – in his haste he had left his overcoat at the Hotel Dobray, where he had been playing billiards with Hunchback Miha into the late afternoon.

The crowd was silent as the shot still echoed in the air, but then, somewhere in the back, whispering started.

'Sugar Neni – that filthy coat is hers.'

'Who?'

'That whore from the Dobray – she wears something like that.'

'It's hers? So she must have been the one who gnawed the face off that poor man!'

'Let's go get her! Bring her here!' people started shouting.

Barbarič, it seemed, was about to lose control of the crowd, which was turning into a lynch mob, but he knew he could not let this happen. This was his first big intervention and if he failed now, he would certainly be tossed out of local government, just as he getting comfortable there.

He again raised the pistol in the air, but now he did not have to fire it; people had somehow calmed down on their own.

'Bring all the evidential materials, the coat and the shoes, to the Dobray,' Barbarič said. 'And take the deceased to the hospital so the doctor can examine him. And then have him placed in the hospital morgue until further notice.'

Everyone finally scattered when the sky over Sóbota lit up with rockets flying across the Mura and falling on the German bunkers. Then, for a long time, there was only whistling, as Stalin's pipe organ, that mysterious weapon of war, again played its music, as if heavenly trumpets were sounding.

The only person on the street was the gravedigger, a man named Gider, but this time he was pushing his handcart not to the cemetery but to the Sóbota hospital.

Waiting for him at the door were Dr Vrbnjak and Comrade Linna, in her high boots; she had been helping at the hospital all week.

3

That Friday – exactly four years after the attack on Yugoslavia, when on April 6, 1941, Hitler's Luftwaffe bombed Belgrade – things unfolded very quickly in Sóbota. It was the eve of the first big rally in honour of the liberators, on a day when people were still dying on the Mura, just as they were on battlefields everywhere.

The whistling and dreadful wail of the rockets, as if the sky was moaning, had not yet ended when Barbarič returned to the Hotel Dobray, where he now played billiards regularly in the evening, although previously he was not often seen at the green tables. The new head of local government had been neither an habitué of coffee houses nor a member of the elite.

Entering behind him were two political activists with the evidential materials – one was carrying the muddy shoes; the other, the ruined coat with the fur collar.

Hunchback Miha had, in fact, returned to town only the day before, on Thursday, April 5, when he led a meeting of the Regional Committee of the Liberation Front. Just a few people in Sóbota knew that he had already been there in late March, for a single night – more precisely, only three people knew this, one of whom was now in the hotel. This was the hotelier, Laci, who was sparing no effort to restore order to the Hotel Dobray. Everything now looked as it had in the old days: downstairs, lots of drinks were being poured; upstairs, people were playing billiards, and the gypsy orchestra had returned, the same one that had run off from the railway station, no one knew where, after Izak's debut concert at the coffee house was cancelled.

But still, Laci thought, everything is different. It's true, the soldiers were gone, but now the people who, again, had essentially moved into the Hotel Dobray had no sense of manners, as he liked to put it; nobody respects anyone any more; suddenly everybody is the same – shoemaker and professor, hotelier and coachman, fiddler and artist, old and young. Thus in the evenings, talking with Sugar Neni, who was the only one who still listened to him, Laci the hotelier would weigh and measure the world through his own spectacles, his own outdated ethics. He consoled himself with the thought that of course a person can never understand everything.

Whether he already knew something, or had heard something, or possibly merely suspected something, or maybe was just listening to 'the voice of the people', about which there was so much talk these days, in any case, Barbarič immediately had two individuals summoned upstairs to the casino: Sugar Neni, a woman who was now merely washing glasses and scrubbing floors at the hotel, and Laci the waiter, as he was called now.

Barbarič was aware that he was acting entirely on his own authority. His true boss, Hunchback Miha, the OZNA agent who had been sent to this forgotten region with special authorization from Ljubljana itself, was at this moment again riding around town on that motorcycle with his drunk associate, as if making sure that all the citizens of Sóbota were sleeping.

It was dark in the casino. The only lamp burning was the one over the billiard table on which Barbarič was positioning the billiard balls. Sugar Neni and Laci were trying to guess, or maybe even suspected, why they had been summoned here – or maybe not.

The balls were now neatly arranged in a triangle.

'Did you hear what was going on outside, in front of the post office?' Barbarič asked, and went over to the cues hanging on the wall.

The other two said nothing, as if they had not heard the question; they were both counting the colourful balls. They felt that something was missing.

'We found a dead man, a disfigured corpse. People are saying you two might know something about it.'

Sugar Neni, still showing no reaction, was gazing absently at the green table, which she knew extremely well, although now she was not thinking about József, who had left her there; she was not thinking anything at all.

'No,' Laci said.

'And you?' Barbarič hissed as he slammed the white cue ball on the table.

She was silent as the grave.

Then Barbarič abruptly leaned over, as if preparing to make the break shot, and lifted the mud-stained coat onto the table with the cue. He dropped it on top of the billiard balls, so it covered them.

'And this?' he asked. 'Do you recognize this fancy coat?'

Sugar Neni flinched, as if somebody had woken her out of a bad dream. She clenched her teeth and stared at the coat with surprised, frightened eyes; of course, she recognized it. She thought immediately of Linna. She had not seen her since the day the girl left the hotel, although she knew exactly where she was. But she thought it would be too dangerous to visit her. For one thing, it wasn't a good idea for a woman to walk through town alone these days, especially not her. For another, Linna was sure to be safe at the hospital; nobody would bother her there. Only where did this coat come from? That's what was gnawing at her. Had something happened to Linna?

'And what about this? Recognize it? Is it yours?' Barbarič was shouting now as he waved one of the ruined shoes on the end of the billiard cue.

They had been her last pair of nice suede shoes, the sort she might never own again.

The woman was still just staring, her face white; it looked like she really did not understand anything. She was trying as fast as she could to put it all together, to see where and what had happened; confused images floated before her eyes: a disfigured corpse, that man had said; the coat and the shoes she had lent to Linna that evening, when she herself had had to lie down on this very table and play dead, which was the only thing that still made József happy. Of course, she could not have known where Linna was going in that coat, whether it was just business or if she had dolled herself up for that poor Kolosváry, who was lying in hospital badly wounded, which was now the only place those two lovebirds could be together.

All of this was clearly expressed on the woman's astonished face, as Barbarič, too, could see, so although she had not said a word, he already believed she had nothing to do with this.

But was this really the whole truth or simply a lie to keep her Linna safe, her last secret, which she hoped to take with her to the grave?

But if Linna had committed some crime and this was the proof, she thought, then I have to protect her.

Laci, too, said nothing, although he at least knew a little more: he had sent Linna out into the night wearing that coat – he was sure of it.

'Yes, it's all mine. Nobody else ever had such a beautiful coat with a fur collar like that, and no other lady would know how to wear those suede shoes!' she said confidently. 'Certainly not that wife of yours!' she sneered in Barbarič's face, and let out a big laugh.

'Damn whore! You'll soon find your God again!'

'Why, I never lost him!'

'Men! Men! Apprehend her!'

Barbarič's two colleagues, who had been standing outside the door the entire time, now burst into the casino.

'You are under arrest, in the name of the people and the town government,' Barbarič recited, although he still did not know the proper words by heart; those he would learn in the coming months.

Sugar Neni was taken that Friday to the Sóbota prison, not far from the hospital. There she awaited the real interrogation.

Barbarič then returned to the Hotel Dobray, where he played a game of billiards by himself. He felt satisfied and, for the first time, was in no hurry to go home. The rally is tomorrow, he smiled to himself, and again arranged the billiard balls on the table.

4

At the Sóbota hospital, the lights in the basement, where the morgue was located, were burning late into the night that Friday.

Dr Vrbnjak did everything at the hospital. He removed gall-bladders and appendixes, treated measles and chickenpox and, especially these past few days, bullet wounds and burns; he was stitching up lacerations as if on a conveyor belt, injuries soldiers had inflicted on each other with knives, pistols and bombs. There were more and more dead in the basement, because there wasn't enough of anything upstairs: bandages, medicine, clean surgical instruments, but especially doctors able to care, as best they could under the circumstances, for this human wretchedness.

So Dr Vrbnjak was all the more pleased to welcome volunteers, whether nurses or orderlies or simply someone to wheel the dead away and keep the records in order in the morgue, where there had already been mix-ups and mistakes in identification. For lying here next to Prekmurians who had died of jaundice, blood poisoning or pneumonia, there were now dead bodies from all over Europe – Russians, Germans, Hungarians, Austrians, Serbs, Poles and even Englishmen – all of whom had been scooped up by the front on one side or the other and thrust mercilessly into this obscure, forgotten corner of the world. Here, in this region between the Mura and the Raba, trapped between the two rivers, in the middle of the plain, the souls of these unfortunates, just weeks before the end of the war, had been overtaken by death. And now in the crowded morgue of the Sóbota hospital, they lay like Everyman, side by side, in peace, in silence, as if all was now settled between brothers.

Linna, as mentioned, had arrived at the hospital right after that senseless shooting in Main Square, when two weary and inebriated armies fired at each other, essentially because of some horses. All during the gunfire and the neighing of those miserable horses, Linna had remained at Ascher's house. Hunchback Miha, however, as soon as the shooting began, ran off and hid somewhere far from the town, returning only yesterday.

When the shooting stopped, she, too, ran out to the street. The first thing she saw were the horses that had been hit – they were lying in the street, gasping for air, crying, their mouths foaming. The rest of the herd had scattered into the narrow lanes, so that Benko's butchers were chasing them all over Sóbota until dark.

At the Hotel Dobray, there had been total confusion. Nobody knew what was happening; the soldiers believed that the Russians were already in town and had surrounded them during the night.

József Sárdy, secretary of the Office of the Special Military Tribunal, in nothing but stockings and a woman's dressing gown, had followed the exchange of fire from the balcony of the hotel, while his Sugar Neni still lay on the billiard table, seemingly dead.

That night he had not hit a single ball; they remained where he had placed them, around the motionless and, for him, nameless female body. Now József merely dressed as fast as he could, pulled his boots onto his sore feet and hurried downstairs.

By then Linna was with her Kolosváry. He lay wounded beneath the window, gazing at the carved horses with no understanding of what had happened.

'Come on, we're leaving! March, you damn swine!' József Sárdy, secretary of the Office of the Special Military Tribunal, shouted at the men. 'What are you waiting for? Can't you see? The Russians will slaughter every one of us! March! Everybody out!'

At that moment Linna grabbed Kolosváry's tunic and covered his face with it.

'He's dead!' she wailed, leaning over his body. She was weeping.

The headless army, with no high command, was running down Main Street towards the Sóbota prison. It was only after they had started retreating that József Sárdy, secretary of the Office of the Special Military Tribunal – who, perhaps, did not bear this rank for nothing – had an idea.

'We're taking the birdies with us. If they're going to fly, we all fly together!'

In less than an hour, they were at Črnske Meje, where they shot the twelve hostages in cold blood. The student Gašparič, a proud Slovene who did not hesitate to say as much at coffee-house tables, sometimes too loudly, was not found until two months later, among the fields to which he had dragged himself, mortally wounded, after having had just one more chance to open his eyes and gaze upon the site of the massacre.

And so, by covering her soldier with his tunic, Linna saved his life. With Laci's help she brought the grievously injured Kolosváry to the hospital. As soon as they arrived, she told Dr Vrbnjak that she would be willing to help in any way she could so long as she could stay with her man, who, she thought to herself, had now been wholly entrusted to her by fate.

'Who are you?' was all Dr Vrbnjak asked.

By evening she was already assisting in the morgue.

5

The telephone had been ringing for a long time before Josip Benko, sitting in the dark in his office, picked up the receiver. He had turned the brass key three times in the lock, but the magic wasn't working now.

He had wanted peace and solitude again, which he had no longer been able to find these past few days; not even that strong Goričko *palinka* did the trick any more.

Now, when all that could be heard were distant explosions and whistling somewhere on the Mura, Benko felt more and more that the peace and freedom they would be celebrating tomorrow only appeared to be real, like a beautiful thought or an illusion in a bottle; maybe he had realized, too, that the spirit of the age, which not so long ago there had been so much talk about over billiards, was not on his side; from the way people spoke to him, looked at him and now, openly, even gave him orders and extorted more and more favours from him, he was feeling like a stranger in his own home, in this *varaš*, which in his own way he had helped to build.

He was sitting in his armchair looking at patches of light on the ceiling. Every so often a motorcycle with a sidecar would speed past his building as it drove round and round the streets of Sóbota. He knew very well who this was, this person who had the gall to circle the streets at night like this, all the while boozing in the sidecar. Hunchback Miha. It pained him every time that light flashed into the office.

'That rally will be the last thing I do for this *varaš*,' he said to himself. Something had finally stirred inside him, as if, without realizing it, he had decided to take a risk, to stand up for himself, whatever the price, the way Mr Josip Benko, company director and large-scale industrialist, former mayor, former member of parliament and, especially, respected husband and father, in short, that distinguished citizen of Sóbota, had always been able to stand up for himself.

But still there was in this decision, this desire, something left unsaid, something he could no longer think about – it was too painful; it must have been smouldering, burning inside him, the way only conscience can burn, for now he was just Benko, even the butchers and foremen called him that; a few more days and there would be no directors here any more, no industrialists, mayors, members of parliament, and Sóbota itself would no longer be the town he had known. All he had left were his devoted wife and the son he had long wished to make peace with.

Now, really for the first time, he felt heartache when he saw how much beauty had been washed downstream; everything, the only thing that was important, he had missed out on, had forgotten on a train that would never be coming back.

'Sir, I am calling from the Dobray,' said a voice, when Benko at last picked up the receiver and put an end to that annoying ringing. He recognized at once the respectful voice of the hotelier, Laci. 'They found a dead body. The postman.' There was a painful pause. 'They also have a lady's dress coat with it. What I'm trying to tell you, sir, is, Sugar Neni is in jail. You're the only one who can help. If not now, it will be too late.'

Everything suddenly was silent again.

His large and luxurious ship, with which he might have conquered the world, had begun to sink. The captain, in his plans, his hopes and even in his faith, was now alone. Everything he had created for himself in all those years of hard work and renunciation – and of course he had, in turn, given so much to this backward, forgotten region, which could not, or did not want to, understand this – it had all been blown away by the wind like fallen leaves from the road.

But there was still time before his ship was swallowed by that invisible Pannonian sea, by this land, which now only blind men were still stubbornly clinging to – there was still a chance to escape, to save himself from the deluge.

People, of course, had tried to persuade him, some had even told him point-blank, that it would be best if he took whatever he could and left, crossed the border somewhere; with his connections, contacts and abilities, he could easily start over again. Until that Friday night, all doors, one might say, had been open to him.

If a short while earlier he had still been thinking, making plans and looking for serious opportunities to leave, to save himself, his business and of course his family, who were all he had left, now he was firmly resolved, with a conviction that was unshakeable, as everybody knew, including his wife and son: he would stay. Here, and no place else, was where he was needed, and he knew that he could help. I still have much to do to put this land on its feet, he told himself.

And, of course, there was still the promise he had made: to get Linna to safety. Her mother (a fact that he alone knew) was already in prison. So it had started, and now nobody was safe any more.

He may not have known everything right then – such as what connection that corpse had with Linna; if it was just a coincidence, or mishap, that they found the coat and shoes Linna had worn that night, as only he and Laci knew; just as they knew that the postman had never appeared again, although nobody had missed him because they were certain he must have joined up with the Partisans, or been mobilized by them – and he had not asked Linna about any of this, but he did know that she was right now at the hospital, with her man.

If there was anything else he knew then, we will never know for sure.

He picked up the heavy receiver again and dialled a number. It was late, nearly eleven o'clock, but the phone did not ring very long.

'Please, it's urgent. Could you come right away to the factory? The spoiled meat needs to be driven out of town.'

Benko could not act on his own; he could no longer drive himself places. The keys to his vehicles had been taken away from him right after the liberation and put at the disposal of the temporary military government with its many committee members, commissars and activists. He had also been assigned a new plant supervisor – Ruslanov, needless to say, had disappeared as soon as the Russians arrived. This was Comrade Karas, who had previously worked as a travelling salesman for the company. Karas, who was now in charge of the keys, also chauffeured officers and government officials around the region, which he knew like the back of his hand.

He was the first person Benko called. Despite the fact that their entire relationship had been stood on its head, they had preserved a mutual respect and trust, which was by no means common these days.

Benko knew that Karas was an honourable man. He had never caused him any difficulty; it was only that envious wife of his who complained. She was always trying to compete with the other Sóbota ladies, but never could – for her, of course, everything was about prestige and money, of which she had never had enough.

Next he called Dr Vrbnjak, with whom he played chess. He had also done him favours: on more than one occasion he had donated meat to the hospital from his factory.

He told Dr Vrbnjak to have Linna and her wounded soldier ready for a long trip. They should wait for him at the back of the

237

hospital, by the exit from the morgue; he made a point of saying that this was all confidential and he mustn't speak of it to anyone. The doctor, of course, understood.

Not long before midnight a van with the words 'Josip Benko Wholesale Meats' painted on the side in big letters was in the entranceway ready to go. Its lights were off, its motor running.

Naturally, it again occurred to Benko that this was probably his last chance to put himself and his family in a car and leave his Sóbota forever.

His wife and son, however, he had left peacefully asleep, and now he sat down alone next to Karas, who was driving.

'To the hospital, quickly.'

They waited a moment in the darkness, checking to make sure that Lendava Road was empty. Benko was thinking mainly about the motorcycle with the sidecar, which was circling the streets, but he did not want to worry Karas with that.

They drove down Lendava Road and turned into Main Street; on the first floor of the Hotel Dobray, which they could see in the distance, the lights were still burning. As they drove past, Benko noticed that the motorcycle was parked in front of the door of the hotel, which made him feel a little calmer.

The town was dark, quiet and seemingly at rest. Everybody is asleep, Benko thought to himself.

Then they turned into Station Road and, accelerating, raced to the hospital. Neither of them spoke.

Only the lights in the basement were burning.

'To the morgue, in the back,' Benko said tersely.

The van, its lights off and motor running, stopped by the basement doors of the Sóbota Hospital. Everything was ready. Linna was standing in a white work coat and high army boots, holding firmly to one end of a stretcher, on which her man was sleeping, maybe dreaming. Benko took the other end. Nobody spoke.

The wounded man was placed in the back of the van with his escort, amid large cuts of horsemeat, which had been prepared for the rally the next day in honour of the liberators.

'Well, that's that,' was all Benko said as he handed a package to Dr Vrbnjak, who asked no questions.

Karas, who had been sitting all this time behind the wheel, drove off as soon the boss (as he still called him) sat down in the van.

The van rumbled down the macadamized road back towards the Hotel Dobray. They had already turned into Main Street when a motorcycle with a sidecar sped past them at full speed in the darkness. Benko held his breath and tried to remain calm. He knew he had needlessly dragged Karas into something that not even he was sure would succeed.

'Where to now, boss?' Karas asked. He could feel they were in a terrible hurry.

'Austria!'

They were now driving past the Hotel Dobray, where the same lights were still burning, only the motorcycle was no longer there.

Linna was looking out of the little window in the back door of the van. She was thinking of Sugar Neni, who by then had been sitting in prison for several hours, accused of murder, although Linna did not know that, and perhaps never would, just as she did not know that this woman, who had been almost like a mother to her (which is what she was then thinking) was now behaving like one. She was protecting her, risking her own life, gambling with it for the sake of her daughter, although she had never found the courage to tell her the truth. Even after they had become close and trusted each other, she had not been able to say: 'Me, Sugar Neni,' (which was not even her real name) 'a girlie, who knows nothing except how to be with men – I am your mother.'

Also: 'This business is the only thing I ever taught you.'

But Linna was happy now, in the hope that she was leaving this town. And how could she not be happy? She had always dreamed of this, that she and her soldier, who was looking at her with those sad eyes of his, would one day be free, that she would feel no shame as they lay together beneath this wide, deep Pannonian sky.

Maybe, if we ever do come back, I'll go to the Hotel Dobray, where I found my new life, and sing.

6

A few minutes after one in the morning, the sky lit up with rockets flying one after the other over the Mura River, only a few miles away.

The whistling of the missiles, which on one side of the river were sowing death, and on the other, mainly fear and anxiety, which burrowed into the souls of the people on the plain, could still be heard as the van stopped on a hidden path by the stream that separated the new Yugoslavia, only now being born, from the old Austria.

The border had not yet been secured, or even fully demarcated – over the coming months, multitudes would flee in terror to the other side, hoping that this was the invisible boundary nobody had yet drawn, the line that separated life from death.

Benko knew they were running out of time.

If they were being followed, and he was almost sure they were, then they had just a few minutes' advantage.

He climbed out of the van; the driver remained behind the wheel with the motor running in the darkness. He helped the wounded man struggle to his feet. He was supporting himself on Linna and a tall crutch.

'Austria is on the other side of that stream. You're refugees now. You'll need to find a ride to Halbenrein – there's a butcher there named Huber; he'll hide you. Wait there until this bloodbath ends. And may God help you. Now, hurry!'

The water made a gentle plash and washed away every trace of the two souls who disappeared into the darkness.

Benko stood there just another moment to light his first cigarette of the night. He inhaled deeply. Then somewhere there was a rustling in the trees, and he heard the startled birds singing what sounded like 'who are you, who are you'. By the time he exhaled the soft, warm smoke, all was quiet again.

7

On Saturday, April 7, 1945, in the courtyard in front of Sóbota Castle, one of the first rallies in honour of the liberators took place. It was quiet along the Mura that morning, although the war would go on claiming its own for another whole month, until May 9, when peace was proclaimed.

In the first row, on chairs that had been brought out from the great hall in the castle, sat officers, representatives from the Liberation Front and a few foreign guests. No Russian soldiers or generals were present.

Hunchback Miha, surprisingly sober and nervous, was pacing around a big pot simmering with horsemeat goulash, which Benko's butchers had prepared. He was keeping an eye on Benko, checking constantly to see where he was. Benko, meanwhile, was calmly and with innate fastidiousness straightening the white tablecloth that covered the long table on which lunch would later be served.

Laci, the hotelier, stood in the background pouring wine, which some Partisans had brought from the Lendava Hills.

Although it was Saturday, the day Franz Schwartz would ordinarily have spent at home with his wife, listening to their son play the violin or simply reading, he had been ordered to be here. Everything is different now and there's nothing I can change, he thought, as if he, too, had come to terms with the situation.

Hope, the only thing that had brought him home, had dwindled away, dissolved like the fog.

At some point during the passionate and forthright speech delivered by Comrade Barbarič, who recalled the difficult road to freedom and listed the many victims, including of course Russians, whose lives this struggle had demanded, and who in a particularly loud voice declared that, now that the war was over, it was imperative to expose and condemn the old elites, the bourgeoisie and the reactionary intelligentsia, to take away everything they have, he cried, so that we the people can use it – that is when Franz Schwartz felt a tug at his sleeve.

It was Edina, the daughter of the tailor, Géza; he recognized her right away. She was by herself – her father was with the Partisans, in Dolenjska, and her mother, who had signed up with the Red Cross, was helping to look for relatives, acquaintances or just good people, who could take in the many children who were now alone or displaced. But all these things the girl told him later, when they were sitting together eating the steaming goulash.

Now all she said was: 'Who is going to heal them, Mr Schwartz?'

'Who do you mean?'

'The dead!'

To Franc Švarc, my grandfather, who never talked about this.

The Author

Dušan Šarotar, born in Murska Sobota, Slovenia, is the author of five novels, three short-story collections, and three books of poetry, as well as a book of essays. He has twice been shortlisted for Slovenia's prestigious Kresnik Award – for the novels *Billiards at the Hotel Dobray* (2007) and *Panorama* (2015). *Panorama*, in English translation, was also shortlisted for the Oxford-Weidenfeld Translation Prize (2017) and longlisted for the Dublin Literary Award (2018) and, in Spanish translation, won the César López Cuadras Readers' Prize (Sinaloa, Mexico, 2017). He has written fifteen screenplays, including the short film *Mario Was Watching the Sea with Love* (based on one of his short stories), which in 2016 won first prize for Best Short Film at the Ningbo (China) Central and Eastern Europe Film Festival as well as a Global Short Film Award (New York). Šarotar is also an acclaimed photographer, whose work has been exhibited at home and abroad. Photographs from his series *Souls* are included in the permanent collection of the Galerija Murska Sobota.

The Translator

RAWLEY GRAU, originally from Baltimore, has lived in Ljubljana since 2001. He has translated numerous works from Slovene, including Dušan Šarotar's novel *Panorama*, which was shortlisted for the 2017 Oxford-Weidenfeld Translation Prize. His other translations include two works by Mojca Kumerdej – the award-winning novel *The Harvest of Chronos* and the short-fiction collection *Fragma* – the novels *Dry Season*, by Gabriela Babnik, *A Chronicle of Forgetting*, by Sebastijan Pregelj, and *The Succubus*, by Vlado Žabot, as well as the short-fiction collection *Family Parables*, by Boris Pintar. He has also translated and edited a collection of poems and letters by the Russian poet Yevgeny Baratynsky, *A Science Not for the Earth*, for which he was awarded the 2016 AATSEEL Prize for Best Scholarly Translation.

Lightning Source UK Ltd.
Milton Keynes UK
UKHW010741290919
350673UK00004B/144/P